TERA LYNN CHILDS

FORGIVE
MY FINS

KATHERINE TEGEN BOOKS
An Imprint of HarperCollins Publishers

Katherine Tegen Books is an imprint of HarperCollins Publishers.

Library of Congress Cataloging-in-Publication Data
Childs, Tera Lynn.
    Forgive my fins / Tera Lynn Childs.—1st ed.
        p.   cm.
    Summary: Seventeen-year-old Lily, half mermaid and half human, has
been living on land and attending high school, where she develops a crush on
a boy but is afraid to tell him of her true destiny as the ruler of the undersea
kingdom of Thalassinia.
    ISBN 978-0-06-191465-2 (trade bdg.)
    [1. Mermaids—Fiction.   2. Princesses—Fiction.   3. Interpersonal
relations—Fiction.]   I. Title.
PZ7.C44185Fo   2010   2009020614
[Fic]—dc22   CIP
                                                                      AC

Typography by Andrea Vandergrift
10 11 12 13 14   CG/RRDB   10 9 8 7 6 5 4 3 2

First Edition

For Sarah, because she took me with her

*W*ater calms me. It's like chocolate or hot tea or dulce de leche ice cream. After a rotten day, I lock the bathroom door, fill Aunt Rachel's old-timey tub with steaming water and bath salts, and then sink into a world where my problems all melt away.

Some days it's not enough.

"Did you ask him?"

Securing the phone against my shoulder, I scoop up a handful of bubble bath and blow the fluff out over my belly. I can choose to ignore the question, right? Especially since neither of us is going to like the answer.

"Lily . . . ," Shannen prods.

When the bubbles hit the water and dissolve into a frothy film, I sigh.

The whole point of this bath was to make me forget my disastrous day—including the subject of Shannen's question—

but that seems impossible. Even though I'm feeling slightly more mellow than when I slid in twenty minutes ago, nothing can completely wash away that memory.

Too bad bath salts can't change the past.

"No," I admit with a frustrated growl. "I didn't ask him."

"I thought we agreed," she says, sounding exasperated. "You were going to ask him in trig when Kingsley had you trade papers."

"We did agree," I concede, "but—"

"But what, Lily?" she interrupts. "You're running out of time."

"I know that." Boy, do I know that. The sand in my countdown timer is draining fast; graduation is just around the corner.

Leaning my head back over the tub's graceful curved edge, I let my hair hang to the floor below. A long mess of blond that defies all attempts at control. I might as well have a sea sponge on my head, since no amount of conditioner or antifrizz serum can tame the effects of Floridian humidity.

"But Kingsley didn't do the normal swap," I explain. "He had us trade down the row instead of across the aisle."

Shannen groans, and I can imagine the look of disgust on her face.

"I hate it when he goes to a professional development workshop," she says. "He always comes back and tries something new that never, ever works."

"I know," I agree, latching on to this divergent train of thought in the vain hope that it will make her—and me— forget our original topic. I'm not above avoidance tactics. I'll totally throw Kingsley under the bus to save myself from another lecture about seizing the day. "It was a total flop." I sit up a little straighter, gaining confidence in my distraction. "The Danfield twins switched places, and most of the class ended up grading their own papers. Kingsley congratulated us on our high grades."

Good grades are a rare thing for me. Shannen's on the valedictorian track and she tries to help me out, but I'm clearly not learning anything by osmosis or association or whatever. Can I help it if all these subjects are like a foreign language to me? My brain just wasn't wired for academic study. The only class I'm pretty sure of passing is art—and only because Mrs. Ferraro likes me. Everything else might as well be advanced nuclear physics.

Besides, lately our unified focus has been on the upcoming Spring Fling dance and not next week's homework. With the dance only days away (as in three), it seems a lot more urgent than an English essay on *Animal Farm*.

Tonight, though, I'd rather talk about homework. Or beauty products. Or swarms of killer jellyfish. Anything other than the thing she's asking about. I fumbled the plan . . . again. The last thing I need right now is Shannen telling me one more time that—

"You're a coward, Lily Sanderson."

—I'm a coward.

Son of a swordfish.

I give my tail fin a flick, sending the key lime bath salts sloshing up over my shoulders. This is the same admonition I've heard every week for the past three years. You'd think I'd get tired of hearing it, suck up my courage, and get it over with. But the trouble is . . . she's right. I am a coward.

Especially where Brody Bennett is concerned.

We mermaids are a cowardly bunch. Keeping our existence a total secret makes cowardice pretty much a necessity. If we don't flee fast enough at the first sign of a passing ship, we might end up on the cover of next week's *Flash Paper*. We're more of an escape-now-ask-questions-later kind of species.

But with Brody it's like I take my flight response to a whole new level of spinelessness. I can make all the plans in the world, be fully ready to follow through, and then the instant he's within sight, I totally clam up. I'm lucky if I'm able to breathe, let alone tell him how I feel. Hormones are cruel like that.

Still, the constant reminder of her cowardice can drive a girl to the edge. For a second—half a second, really—I consider blurting out the one thing I *know* will derail her lecture permanently.

But I've heard the stories.

I know what happens when a human finds out a mermaid

is a mermaid. I love Shannen like a sister, but I can't take that risk. I can't put myself, my family, and my entire kingdom in jeopardy for the sake of avoiding an unpleasant conversation. No matter how badly I want to confess, my duty comes before our friendship.

Shannen would understand.

So, instead of blurting out my dirty little secret—actually, not so dirty at the moment, since my fins are currently gleaming green and gold in the salty water—I resort to the pathetic truth.

"I tried, Shan." My head drops back against the porcelain tub with a well-deserved *thud*. "Really I did. This time I was super, super close. I took a deep breath, said his name, and . . ."

"And what?"

"Quince Fletcher threw a wad of paper at my forehead."

It had taken every last ounce of my self-control—and the dismissal bell—to keep from leaping out of my seat, apologizing to Brody as I vaulted over him, and pummeling Quince into seaweed salad. Merfolk are a peaceful people, but that boy makes me wish I had free reign of Daddy's trident for a good five minutes. I've fantasized some pretty creative ways to shut Quince up.

"That dog," Shannen says. "You'd think it was his self-appointed mission to make your life miserable."

"I know, right?" I rub the shower pouf absently over my scales. "Why does he even bother? I mean, it's like his two hobbies are working on that disaster of a motorcycle and tormenting me."

Thing is, I don't even know why he is so devoted to tweaking me on a near-constant basis. It's not like I've ever done anything to him, other than move into the house next door. At first we were almost friends . . . until he started treating me like the enemy.

Boys aren't nearly so confusing in the ocean.

"He needs to"—a *beep-beep* interrupts Shannen's response—"diversify."

"Hold on." I wiggle myself into a semisitting position. "There's another call."

Aunt Rachel got tired of my bathwater frying the circuits of the upstairs phone about three phones ago. The latest replacement doesn't even have Caller ID, and she swears that this is the last one. Ruin this one and there's no more phone in the tub. So I'm very careful not to lose my grip as I hold out the receiver and press the button.

"Hello?"

"You should check the curtains before you take a bath, princess," a deep, mocking voice says.

"Wha—" I half scream, half yelp as I bolt up in the tub.

The nearest towel is folded neatly on the toilet . . . on the far side of the room. With a powerful kick I flop myself over the side, onto the cold tile floor, and dive for the towel. I am just tossing it over my fins when I hear a roar of laughter coming from the receiver. Scowling, I snatch it off the floor.

"Priceless," he howls, still laughing. "You never fail to amuse, princess."

Aaarrgh! I slam the handset repeatedly on the floor, in what I hope are eardrum-damaging whacks.

"Why?!?" My flipper-fast heartbeat ebbs toward normal as I stare, first at the phone—which has suffered a few nicks from my display of rage—then at the tightly drawn curtains covering the bathroom window. Holding the phone back up to my ear and ignoring the laughter still echoing through the earpiece, I ask, "Why do you enjoy torturing me so much?"

"Because," Quince manages between laughs, "you make it so easy."

Grabbing a handful of now-soaking towel, I throw it against the wall next to the door and watch it slowly slide down into the hamper. Aunt Rachel's cat, Prithi, meows in complaint from her position outside the door.

"You," I say as I pull myself back up onto the edge of the tub, "are a vile"—turning, I sink gingerly into the water—"repulsive"—even lukewarm, it feels heavenly—"slimy-headed vent worm."

I catch the phone against my ear before spreading my hands beneath the water to bring the temperature back up to a Zen-inducing near-steaming.

He chuckles once more before answering, "That's a new one."

"I've got dozens more where that came from," I assure him as I sink back against the wall of the tub and close my eyes. "Care to hear some?"

The salty water envelops me, calming my electrified nerves. Slightly.

"Someday," he says, "I might take you up on that offer."

"Fraidy-fish," I mutter, closing my eyes and imagining I'm back home, the warm currents of the Gulf Stream swirling around me as I float beneath my favorite spot of ocean—the shallow bank just east of Thalassinia where a forest of sea fans and staghorn coral gives me the camouflage I need so I can lie for hours, watching the colorful fishing boats pass above.

That spot is my bliss. I've never taken anyone there, not even Daddy. I'm saving it for someone special. I'm saving it for Brody.

When I feel homesick, I picture us there.

"Admit it, princess," Quince says in what I can only imagine he thinks of as a teasing voice, "you'd be bored without me."

"Without you," I reply, wishing there were more than fourteen feet and two panes of glass separating me from neighbor boy, "I'd have a date to the Spring Fling."

Sudden silence. The base of my neck prickles.

"A date?" he demands.

My eyes flash open.

I hadn't meant for that to slip out. The reheated water relaxed me *too* much. I can't let my guard down for a second when I'm talking to Quince.

"You're not still panting after that Benson boob, are you?"

"Bennett," I snap before I can catch myself. Then, "I don't know what you're talking about."

"I think you do—"

"In fact," I say decisively, "I don't know why I'm still talking to you."

"You're talking to me," he says before I can click back over to Shannen, "because I can help you snag your crush."

"Ha!" I say, brilliantly. Then I follow it up with some hysterical laughter. As if the bane of my existence would ever help me. As if he *could*. "Nice try, Quince."

"Fine." He *tsk*s, as if I've made a poor choice. "When you're ready for help, you know where to find me."

Yeah, in the house next door, peeping on me in the bathroom.

"I wish I didn't," I say. "Hey! How did you know I was in the bath, anyway?" Silence from the pervy end of the line. "Hello?"

Damselfish! I wanted to be the one to hang up on him this time.

The phone beeps, letting me know that Shannen is still waiting on the line. I should have known she wouldn't give up. We haven't finished with the whole asking-Brody-to-

9

the-dance thing. She never misses an opportunity to let me know how I've screwed up and how I can improve myself next time.

I'd wonder why I still speak to her if she weren't my best human friend.

I click over.

"I'm back."

"Who was it?"

"Nobody," I answer, meaning it.

"Quince." It's not a question.

"Whatever," I say, slapping my fin absently against the far wall of the tub. "Just get on with chastising me so I can go to bed."

Shannen ignores my pouty comment. "What did he want?"

"What does he ever want? To bug the carp out of me."

I'm not about to tell her about his offer—or about his spying on me from his bathroom. After three years of living next door to the pervert, I've stopped begging my aunt to move. In a few short weeks I'll be heading back to Thalassinia to complete my education, learning how to rule at my father's side. I'll never have to see or hear him again. He'll be nothing more than a distant—nightmarish—memory.

"He must have wanted something in partic—"

Not in the mood to discuss Quince, I turn back to the subject I know will derail her. "I think I'll ask Brody before school tomorrow."

She switches tracks instantly. "You'd better," she warns. "Time is running out. The dance is on Friday."

"Yes, I—"

"That's three days away."

"I know that." I sit up, twisting around and slipping against the porcelain as I pull the plug out of the drain. "But since he just broke up with Courtney, I don't think he's exactly had time to troll for and reel in a replacement."

I can practically feel her heavy sigh.

"I'm too tired to argue with your fishy phraseologies," she says. "Have you decided what you're going as?"

The water swirls slowly down the drain, leaving a fine film of salty soap on my skin and scales as it sinks. "No," I answer as I cup some water up over my chest to rinse off. "I told you, I'm not going in costume. It's stupid. I'm not a g—" I stop myself from saying "guppy." Even after three years it's hard to keep my sea slang in check. "I'm not a little kid."

"You have to," Shannen insists. "It's a costume dance. A Seaview tradition."

"I'll think of something," I say, just to pacify her.

The water gurgles as the last inch starts to disappear down the drain.

"It has to fit with the Under the Sea theme."

"No, it—"

"I've got it," Shannen shouts, excitement ringing in her voice. "I know exactly what you should be."

"Really?" I ask absently, grabbing the washcloth draped over the side of the tub and wiping the traces of soap film off my scales. "What?"

"You should go as"—she pauses dramatically—"a mermaid."

I drop the phone. Then quickly scramble to get it out before the remaining half inch of water fries its circuits. Aunt Rachel will never buy another one.

"No," I say as water drips off the phone and I hear the distinct sound of snapping electricity. "No, that wouldn't work."

"Think about it. We could *both* go as mermaids," she says. "We'll talk at lunch tomorrow."

I set the still-dripping phone on the base, its cords stretched under the bathroom door to the jack in the hall, and sink back against the empty tub.

Forgetting Shannen and Quince and Brody—well, I can never entirely forget Brody—I focus on my transfiguration. Most of the time I shift between forms without much thought. But when I'm away from the sea, I use my powers less and less. Reheating my bathwater. Chilling my morning juice. Transfiguring for my bath a few times a week. Nothing like when I'm home. Sometimes it makes me feel closer to home to focus on feeling the transition.

Drawing on the magical powers of my people—powers granted by Poseidon's sea nymph Capheira, our ancient ancestor—I picture my iridescent scales dissolving completely away and pale pink skin appearing in its place. Why couldn't I be lucky enough to be born with a tan?

Still, it feels good to have my legs back. After spending the first fourteen years of my life with fins, it's amazing how comfortable I am in terraped form. Three years on land and I feel like I was born to it. I suppose that's because Mom was human.

I wonder what she would think of me, lying here in her sister's bathtub, dreaming about the boy I love. Would she be proud? Disappointed? Glad I'm embracing my human half? I guess I'll never know.

As I wiggle my lime-green-tipped toes, I hear a hiss and a loud *crack* . . . just before the lights go out.

Prithi meows.

"Lily," Aunt Rachel shouts from down the hall. "Have you been using the phone in the bathtub again?"

Covering my face with my hands, I wonder if I never should have left the sea in the first place. High school may be great for humans, but it's no place for a mermaid.

2

*N*othing escapes the scrutiny of a bathroom mirror. Especially first thing in the morning. Especially under the compact fluorescent glow of Aunt Rachel's fixtures.

The harsh lighting washes out my already pale skin, making the freckles painted across my nose and shoulders stand out in the contrast. My blond sea sponge looks more like a halo of yellow cotton candy than hair.

I tug open my makeup drawer, sending the trays of tubes and compacts crashing to the front. Makeup application must be something human girls learn in kindergarten, because after three years of practice the only product over which I have any control is lip gloss. Even that doesn't always go as planned.

I twist off the cap of shimmery pink and swipe the wand over my lips.

"Lily," Aunt Rachel shouts up from downstairs. "You have

a message from your father."

Startled, I lose control of the wand, jerking a gooey pink streak across my cheek before dropping the wand down the front of my shirt and onto Prithi's furry back.

Great. Two hours spent choosing the perfect go-to-the-dance-with-me outfit, and now I have to change.

"Be right down," I shout back, peeling the wand out of Prithi's fur and rinsing it off in the sink. Thankfully, most of the gloss smeared onto my shirt, so there's not much stuck to her.

After a quick glance at the curtain-covered window—maybe I should staple the curtains in place—I tug my navy blue scoop-neck tee over my head. I duck across the hall and grab a last-minute replacement top. I'm just bouncing down the stairs when I hear Aunt Rachel say, "Good morning, Quince. What brings you over?"

I freeze. What is he doing here? Hovering outside the kitchen door, I listen.

"The paper boy misfired again."

I steal a peek and see him handing Aunt Rachel her *Seaview Times*. I don't buy it. He's not that nice. He's probably here with some great new plan for my humiliation. Prithi catches up with me and proceeds to weave figure eights around my ankles. Well, I'm not about to stand around hiding like Lily the cowardly lionfish. Straightening my shoulders, I step around the doorjamb and walk into the kitchen.

"Morning, Aunt Rachel." I give her a smile as I cross to

the counter and pour myself a glass of orange juice. The carton's been out for a while, so I wrap my hand around the tumbler and chill the contents.

As far as I care, Quince isn't even in the room.

"Quince brought over our paper," she explains. "It was accidentally delivered to their porch again."

I snort. Quince probably grabbed it off *our* porch and just pretended to bring it over. To camouflage his true motives. That would be just like him.

"Would like you some breakfast, Quince?" she offers, unfolding the paper and starting in on her morning read. "Lily, why don't you pour a second glass of juice?"

I'm just about to tell him where he can stick his glass of juice when he says, "I already ate, Ms. Hale."

I nearly spill my freshly chilled juice. It's so unlike him to pass up an opportunity to bug me for an extended period of time. When I spin around to figure out why, he's standing right in front of me.

"But," he continues, watching me with his annoyingly Caribbean blue eyes, "I would love a glass of juice."

Why does he of all people have to have eyes the exact color of Thalassinian waters? Teeth clenched, I turn back around and quickly splash some juice into a glass. I shove it at him.

"Here."

"Thanks." He takes the glass—apparently not noticing that I've accidentally chilled it to the point of frost—but doesn't step back. Just downs the ice-cold juice in one chug. He flashes that arrogant grin. "Just what I needed."

"Good," I snap. "Then you can——"

My suggestion that he go take a flying leap out the door dies in my throat when his gaze shifts to my mouth. His smile transforms into more of a smirk as he slowly lifts a hand to my cheek. I'm frozen. What on earth is going on here?

He rubs his fingertips across my skin, then holds them up to inspect.

"Looks like you missed the mark, princess."

Turning his hand, he shows me the smear of shimmery pink gloss he wiped off my face.

"Aaargh!" I growl in frustration, and shove him as hard as I can.

Of course, I forget the glass of juice still in my hand and wind up spilling it all over both of us. He just throws back his head and laughs.

Prithi hisses at Quince. Good girl.

"Lily," Aunt Rachel admonishes. "What were you thinking?"

Before I can defend myself—anyone who hears my side of the story would totally call my actions justified—he says, "It was my fault, Ms. Hale." He winks at me. "I had it coming."

Then, turning to Aunt Rachel, he says, "Mom wanted me to thank you for the organic lemon bars. They were delicious, as always." He grins. "We finished them in a day."

Aunt Rachel blushes. "I'll have to make some more."

She's always sending over stuff like cookies and casseroles to Quince and his mom. One time I asked her why, and she gave me some cryptic answer about neighbors helping neighbors, which I eventually figured out meant Quince's mom struggles to pay the bills with her minimum-wage factory job. They're like the poster family for single mom and deadbeat dad. Aunt Rachel might not be much better off with her pottery studio, but she likes to share her bounty.

"I wouldn't talk you out of it, ma'am." His smile turns sweet, the rotten faker. "See you at school, princess."

Leaving Aunt Rachel beaming and me scowling, he walks out the back door. How does he manage to do this *every time*? I wind up feeling like an idiot, and he comes off looking like a perfect angelfish.

"Nice boy," Aunt Rachel mutters, returning to her paper. "Strange . . . but nice."

My thoughts exactly. Only instead of nice, I'd say awful.

The damp sticky of fresh orange juice finally seeps through my top.

"Ugh, I have to go change." I glance down at my outfit. "Again."

I turn to head back upstairs when Aunt Rachel says, "Don't forget your father's message."

Right. Daddy's message.

I had forgotten, what with the whole Quince thing and the juice and—

"Wait," I blurt as a thought occurs. "Quince didn't see the, uh . . ." I make a wavy gesture at the pale green curl of kelpaper, a waterproof parchment made from wax and seaweed pulp, sitting on the kitchen table.

"What?" Aunt Rachel peers around the newspaper, looking confused. Then the light dawns. "Oh. No, he didn't. The messenger gull was gone before he arrived."

Well, that's one thing in a row that's not a complete disaster. It's not like I could exactly explain a seagull showing up at our kitchen window with a message tied to his leg. Especially not when that message is sealed with the royal crest of the king of Thalassinia.

And, thankfully, the fact that Prithi had been upstairs fixating on me at the time means we didn't have to deal with claws and feathers in the kitchen.

I grab the message and stick it in my bra before rushing upstairs to find backup outfit number three. Maybe my one-item-long run of luck will continue with the Brody plan.

"Morning, Brody," I say, trying to act like I haven't been waiting for twenty minutes, knowing he would be in before school to check on the news-team footage we shot yesterday. He slips into the chair next to me at the editing station.

Without looking up from the screen playing raw film from his latest newscast, he says, "Hey, Lil."

My heart quivers. Every time I hear his voice, I feel like I've just had a brush with an electric eel. Little sparks of energy tingle along all my nerves, sending them into total shock. Which might explain why I lose all ability to form coherent thoughts, let alone actual comprehensible speech.

With his attention fully focused on the editing screen, I indulge in a few seconds of unnoticed worship—er, observation. After three years, I know every feature by heart. Curving lips that would make Cupid proud, always spread in an I'm-the-king-of-the-world kind of smile. Lusciously curly hair, the color of Hershey's Extra Dark, that is more often than not still damp from early-morning swim practice. His eyes aren't like any I've ever seen, a pale golden brown that glows when he looks at you straight on.

Which doesn't usually happen to me.

But that's going to change. Because I have a plan. And a very important question to ask. Right now.

"The tape looks good," I offer, hoping to get his focus off the screen for a second.

"Yeah . . . ," he says, not sounding real happy. He picks up a headset and holds one side up to his ear like a singer in a recording studio. My heart trips again. "Why does my voice sound so tinny?"

He still hasn't looked at me.

"Oh," I say in a voice as confident as I can manage—aka *not very* around Brody. "There was some feedback on the new mics. Ferret will fix it in post."

"Great," he says as he tosses the headset on the table and swivels to face me.

His smile makes me dizzy—in a good way. I know this is love. What else could make me sweat and smile and swoon all at once?

If only he would realize this.

Of course, that will never happen if I don't ask the question. Right now.

"So . . . ," I start hesitantly. "Are you going to the—"

"You have beautiful eyes, Lil." He tilts his head to the side, as if trying to get a better look. Or as if he's just noticing for the first time that I actually *have* eyes.

I feel the blush burn my pale cheeks, even though I know not to get too excited. Brody throws out comments like that all the time. At first I thought it meant he liked me, but he does that to everyone. It's part of his charm.

Certain I look like a red-cheeked clown fish, I swallow over the lump in my throat and try to continue.

"I know you and Courtney broke up," I begin again. "But I was wondering if—"

"Yeah, finally." He leans back in the chair, folds his arms behind his neck, and looks at the ceiling. "I was tired of her nagging. Always harping at me to buy her flowers or cut my hair or change my clothes. Can't believe I put up with it for two whole years."

Me neither.

Then again, I've been the one listening to his complaints

for the last twenty-two months. I never could understand why he went out with her in the first place. She made him take her to La Piscina on their first date. He shelled out eighty bucks and she ended the night by slapping him. (Just because he didn't get out to walk her to her door.)

But that's all over now. *They're* over. It's my turn. Right now!

I have no excuses left, and Spring Fling is the perfect opportunity. Not too formal or too much of a social commitment, like prom or homecoming would be. Just two friends (are we friends?) hanging out, dancing, and drinking weak lemonade. Nothing intimidating about that, right?

Then why are my hands shaking like a sea fan in a hurricane?

Finally, dredging the depths for my last few drops of courage, I ask, "Do you want to go to the dance wi—"

"Well, well, well," a deep voice calls from the doorway. "You two lovebirds should just hook up and get it over with. All this tension gives me hives."

My cheeks erupt in flames.

"Good one, Fletcher," Brody says, laughing. He elbows me in the ribs like Quince just told the funniest joke. "As if Lil would have any interest in a ladies' man like me."

Quince fills the doorway, arms crossed over his chest like some muscle-bound action hero. And, I think with a little pride, wearing a different shirt from the one I juiced earlier. He stares at me with those clear steady eyes, dark blond brows raised, silently daring me to say something.

I stare right back.

"Yeah," I say, forcing half a laugh. "As if."

While Quince and I continue our staredown—to Brody's complete oblivion—the school bell rings.

"Gotta go." Brody grabs his backpack and heads for the door. At the last second he turns and asks, "What were you going to ask me, Lil?"

The side of Quince's mouth lifts in a little smirk. But—much to my shock—he doesn't say a word of what I know is running through his mind. He just holds my stare, daring me to ask Brody right in front of him.

An audience is the last thing I need.

I can just imagine the humiliation that would bring. Especially if Brody says no. Which he probably will. I mean, he sees me as a pal. A news-team buddy and swim-team manager. *Maybe* he's noticed I'm a girl—I'm not completely devoid in the topside department—but I'm sure he's never thought of me like that. As a girl who might be interested in a boy. In him.

He'll probably laugh in my face.

If he's going to give me the big letdown, I'd rather do this audience-free.

Unwilling to concede the staredown to Quince, I answer Brody without looking away. "I'll, uh, ask you later."

23

"Sure," he says. "See ya, Fletcher."

"Yeah," Quince says, smiling. "Later." Then he winks at me.

That is the last straw.

As Brody slips out the door—heading for his first-period class, economics—I launch out of my chair and attack Quince with a howl of frustration.

"Aaargh!" I try to pummel him with my fists, but he grabs me by the wrists and easily holds me back. "Why?" I shout. "Why do you enjoy ruining my life?"

I keep yelling at Quince, struggling against his solid grip. Working on motorcycles must build muscles, because he looks like he's not even trying hard to keep me from beating the carp out of him.

I swear, I never used to be this violent. Mermaids are always a little more hot-blooded on land, but whenever I'm around *him*, I just want to break things. Starting with his nose—

"Chill, princess," he says in that annoyingly soothing voice. "I just saved you from making a huge mistake."

That gets my attention.

"Excuse me?"

"Asking Benson to the dance just then—"

"Bennett," I correct automatically.

"—would have gotten you a big fat no."

I hold my fury for about three seconds before I slump. Great. It's bad enough to know deep down that your dream guy doesn't want you, but to have an outsider say the same thing really sucks seaweed.

Okay, so maybe I'm not a knockout cheerleader like Courtney. My nose is a little on the longish side and my pale skin will never take a tan—sun exposure is pretty limited in the deep blue sea. My hair is, as previously lamented, a disaster. My curves aren't totally lacking, but they're not lingerie-catalog-worthy. I've got too many freckles, my eyes are too big, and I have the coordination of a giant octopus. Maybe Quince is right. I could never—

"Don't do that," he says, as if sensing my train of thought, his voice softer. "Don't twist my words."

"What is that supposed to mean?"

"I wasn't saying you have no chance with him." He finally releases my wrists and steps back. "You're too good for a loser like him."

"Then what," I bite out, ignoring his second comment, "were you saying?"

"Asking him to the dance is not the way to catch his attention."

"Oh really," I snap. "What do you know about it?"

"I know," he says, lowering casually into one of the editing chairs like he belongs, "that he's not looking for a date."

"And just how would you know that?"

"Courtney."

"Right." I drop into my chair. "Why would she tell you anything?"

He stretches his long, jeans-hugged legs out in front of

him and sets one biker boot on top of the other. "Some girls actually *enjoy* talking to me."

"Only ones with jellyfish for brains," I mutter.

"Anyway," he continues, "when Bens——"

When I start to correct him, he holds up a hand and backtracks.

"When Bennett broke up with her, he said he wanted to be single for a while, taste the fruits of freedom and all that garbage. He'll be going stag to the dance."

I roll my eyes. As if I believe anything this sea slug says.

"Ask him, then," he says.

"I will."

"Don't say I didn't warn you."

I stand, grabbing my backpack and slinging it over my shoulder. "I won't."

The tardy bell rings as I step out into the hall. *Damselfish!* One more tardy to American government and it'll drop my already precarious grade. Yet another thing I can blame on Quince Fletcher.

3

"*G*o now!" Shannen shoves me out of the lunch line. "Before the goons behind us get to his table."

Glancing over my shoulder, I see that she's right. Brody's posse—the swim team and cheerleading squad—are in line behind Shannen, behind the spot I just occupied. Out in the cafeteria, Brody is sitting alone at their table.

If I'm going to ask him, I'd better do it now. It's my best chance.

With a deep breath, I hand my lunch to Shannen, push my way through the crowd around the registers, and make my way to Brody's table. He doesn't notice right away when I approach, so I clear my throat. He looks up and all the words in my mind wash away. He's like high tide, clearing out my thoughts as easily as driftwood on the beach.

For a moment I'm back to the first time I saw him. It

was the afternoon before my first day at Seaview High. The nerves and the fears and the homesickness had gotten to me. I was a mermaid, a girl of the sea! What was I thinking, going to terraped high school? I'd never survive.

So I'd left Aunt Rachel a note and headed for the beach. Leaving my clothes under the pier, I'd slipped beneath the water, intent on swimming home.

Then there was a splash in front of me, and when the bubbles cleared, I saw a boy gliding beneath the waves. He was clearly human, but he swam like he belonged in the water. Like he *was* the water.

That was the moment I knew. If a terraped boy could feel that at home in the water, surely I could survive a few months on land. After all, I was half human. And I wanted to find out more about my mom's world.

That was also the moment I fell in love with Brody. He's the reason I've stayed in Seaview for all of high school, instead of the one year I'd originally planned. He's my future mermate.

Of course, when I was little, I never imagined I'd be bringing a human boy home to meet Daddy, but I'm pretty confident Daddy will see that Brody's meant to be in the water. And Brody will love Thalassinia.

It's way past time I finally tell him how I feel.

Smiling, he says, "Hey, Lil." He forks a bite of pasta into his mouth. "What's up?"

"Um," I say, my voice suddenly quivering like an electric

eel on full volts. "About what I was going to ask you this morning."

"Right." He swallows his food and takes another bite. "Shoot."

"Well, I just—"

"Hey, is this about that special report on price gouging in the school vending machines?" His brows drop to shadow his golden-brown eyes. "I verified my numbers with three independent snack food distributors."

I love that he is so dedicated to his work and excited about this exposé, but is a nickel a candy bar really price gouging?

"Actually, it's about Spring Fling," I blurt. "Since you and Courtney broke up, I was wondering if you might want to . . ."

My question trails off when I see his eyes soften with something that looks dangerously like sympathy. No, no, no. Not a good sign.

He sets down his fork and stands up.

"Oh, Lil," he says, sounding sincerely sad. "You know I love you, but—"

No phrase in the history of civilization that begins with "I love you, but . . ." has ever ended well.

"Sure," I say quickly, eager to get my humiliation over with. "No problem." Tears prickle at the back of my eyes. "Forget I asked."

I turn to rush away, but Brody grabs my arm.

"Listen," he says, pulling me back to face him. "I need

some time on my own right now. To find out what I really want for the first time in two years. It wouldn't be fair to you—or any girl—if I said yes."

Whatever. He's just too nice to say he'd never in a million billion years go with someone like me.

"Of course," I say, sniffing, hoping my tears don't well up beyond the point of surface tension. "I totally understand."

And I totally need to get out of here. Breaking into tears in the school cafeteria only leads to one thing: gossip. Most of the school already thinks I'm part freak. I don't need to feed the swell.

"Hey," he says, reaching for my chin and tilting my head up. "Save me a dance."

I smile weakly.

"Promise," he says, flashing me his most charming smile.

I nod. Then the table is suddenly surrounded by jocks and swishing poms. Taking advantage of the crowd, I slip away and head for the nearest restroom.

I don't know what's worse: that Brody said no, or that Quince told me he would. Why does he always have to be right?

Because it's lunchtime, the halls are empty and I make it to the girls' bathroom without being seen. In a back stall I succumb to several long minutes of crying. I feel like someone pulled out my still-beating heart, stomped on it a few times with dirty motorcycle boots, and then shoved it back into my chest. All the fears that kept me quiet for three long years were just publicly unveiled. Brody will never love me. The whole reason I stayed on land just evaporated like sea foam on sand.

Eventually my tears dry out. My eyes are red and puffy. At least they're not glittering gold like they would be underwater. Still, no amount of cold water splashes gets them back to normal. They're a flashing neon sign shouting, "She just cried her eyes out in the bathroom!" I almost start to cry all over again when I realize that everyone is going to wonder what's wrong. Everyone who hasn't already heard the tale of my humiliation, that is.

Then a thought occurs. Shannen wears contacts. I bet she has some eyedrops in her locker.

Dabbing the water off my face, I head out in the direction of her locker.

And walk smack into Quince Fletcher.

"Believe me now?" he asks.

He's leaning casually against the wall just outside the girls' bathroom. From the arrogant look on his face, I can guess he's been waiting for me so he can gloat.

"Get lost."

I try to walk around him, but he sidesteps and blocks my path.

"Move!"

"I asked you a question."

"And I choose not to answer." I step to my left, and he

mirrors me. Back to the right. He follows.

Why won't he leave me alone? What did I ever do to deserve his obnoxious attentions?

Guess my tears aren't dried up after all. They're right back at the ready and threatening to spill out if Quince doesn't let me go.

"Admit it," he insists. "I was right."

"No." I sniff. "You were wrong." *Sniff.* "I'm just crying" —*sniff*—"'cause I'm so happy." My tears take that lie as their cue and start streaming down my cheeks.

"Come on, princess," he says. "You don't need to cry over that loser."

This only makes me cry harder. We both know who the loser is in this scenario.

With a muttered curse, Quince wraps his arms around me and squeezes. It feels remarkably like a hug.

"Don't cry," he whispers in my ear. "Please."

I don't know if it's his soft words or the fact that my face is now hidden by his broad chest, but I just let go. Three years of longing and loving from a distance have built to the breaking point, and I let it out all over his West Coast Choppers T-shirt.

"*Shhh*," he soothes. "He's not worth it."

Sob, sob, sob.

I can't stop. I've totally lost control of my emotions. All I can think is, Brody hates me and I'm stuck seeking comfort from my worst enemy. My life has definitely sunk to the deepest dregs.

Faintly, muffled by Quince's chest and the sound of my tears, I hear a bell. It only vaguely registers as the end of lunch.

Quince curses, and the next thing I know I'm moving against my will, back into the bathroom and into a small, enclosed space.

Through swollen, tear-blurred eyes I see that we are in a bathroom stall. The sound of giggling echoes on the sterile white tile a split second before Quince sits on the toilet and pulls me onto his lap.

"Lift your feet!" he whispers urgently. I obediently brace the soles of my flip-flops against the stall door.

Two pairs of high heels walk past, clacking loudly on the tile floor.

"Did you see her run out of the cafeteria?" one girl asks, her voice gleeful.

"I bet he put her in her frizzy-haired place."

My stomach rolls.

Maybe they're talking about some other frizzy-haired girl who got humiliated at lunch today. Seaview High is a big school. Surely someone else—

"As if a freak like her could ever tempt Brody Bennett."

Nope. Me.

Those rotten tears—momentarily startled away—spill down my cheeks.

"She needs to learn to keep her paws off another girl's

guy," the first voice says.

I gasp. "It's Court—"

Quince's hand clamps over my mouth. His other arm is wrapped around my waist, and he uses both to tug me back tight against his chest. "*Shhh*," he whispers super quietly in my ear.

I nod, wondering how I got myself into this position and hoping my agreement will make Quince release me. It doesn't.

"She has the fashion sense of a palm tree," the other girl says.

"Oh, come on," Courtney—aka Brody's newly ex— replies, and I think she's about to defend me. "A palm tree at least wears coordinating colors."

Through a teary blur, I glance down at my clothes. I don't see anything wrong with my pale yellow T-shirt and turquoise ruffled skirt. And my bright pink flip-flops match the hearts on my tee. Granted, this was my Plan C for the day, but I didn't think it was that bad.

"Pink and yellow?" Courtney continues. "What does she think she is? A walking candy shop?"

The other girl—probably Courtney's constant sidekick, Tiffany—laughs. "At least she makes an effort. That's more than you can say about her friend."

My ears perk up, and I have instantly forgotten my humiliation. No one talks about Shannen around me without getting an earful of back-in-your-face.

34

"The one whose entire wardrobe consists of jeans and polo shirts?" Courtney's voice is filled with acid. "Someone should tell her they sell my castoffs at Goodwill."

That does it.

I lurch forward, grabbing for the latch and dropping my feet to the floor. Quince has lightning-fast reflexes, though. Before my fingertips connect with metal, he closes over my arms and tightens them back against me. His legs shoot out, wrapping around my ankles and slipping back into place so that anyone looking into the stall will see only his jeans and boots.

"Don't," he whispers almost silently against my ear. "She's not worth it."

I consider this for a second, deciding that he's probably right—no matter how badly I hate admitting that. Courtney's probably still mad that Brody dumped her right before the dance. I can let her horrid comments slide. Then, as I relax a little and absorb the sudden silence, something disturbing happens. I start to notice things. Weird, unsettling things.

Like how warm Quince's chest feels against my back.

And how his breath tickles my ear, sending shivers down my spine.

And how his arm is resting just below my chest.

The total silence must be playing tricks on my mind, because for a second—half a second, really—I almost think his touch feels goo—

His arm tightens, quick and sharp, around my belly.

"*Uungh*," I grunt.

Why on earth did he—

"*Ew*," Courtney whines.

Oh, great. Now I'm more than humiliated. . . . I'm constipated.

Thankfully, before things can get worse—I can't imagine how, but I'm sure they could—the tardy bell rings and they finally make their way, heels clacking across the floor, to the door.

As they leave, I hear Tiffany say, "Did you see the boots in that stall?"

"Yes," Courtney scoffs, and raises her voice. "Must be that butch girl from the football team. Doesn't she have a mother?"

God, Courtney is such a sea witch.

Their voices trail off, and Quince and I are left in the quiet of an empty bathroom. Still, he doesn't release me.

Maybe he's mad at what she said about his boots.

Though for the life of me I can't figure out why, I feel compelled to make him feel better. "Your boots aren't *that* bad. You know she thought you were Em—"

Before I can finish, he bursts out laughing, nearly shaking me off his lap and onto the disgusting bathroom floor.

"Wha—" I squeal as I slide off to the left.

His arms tighten around me, securing me in place. After a few more seconds of holding on for dear life while Quince indulges in some seriously rumbling laughter against my back, he finally releases me and helps me stand.

"Sorry, princess," he says, still sitting on the toilet. "That was just too damn funny."

Twisting around in the tight space, I glare at him. "Well, I'm glad you found humor in your humiliation. I don't happen to enjoy being ridiculed and—"

"Aw, come on," he teases, an annoyingly bright grin shining on his tan face. He's got one of those strong faces that completely transform with a smile. Dark and foreboding one second, fun and playful the next. "Couldn't you see through her?"

I must look confused, which I am, because he explains, "She's jealous."

"Right," I say, thinking back to the cafeteria. "I'm plucking Brody right out from under her perfectly sculpted nose."

Squeezing up against one wall, I try to open the stall door. I need to escape, to get out into the open, away from him. Only the stall is so small and Quince takes up so much space that I can't open it while he's sitting on the toilet.

"Stand up."

He complies but stays in front of the door. Hovering over me, he says, "Hard as it is to believe, I won't say 'I told you so' about the dance."

As if.

"In fact," he says, leaning over me to brace his forearm on the wall above my head, "I'm going to help you out."

At the moment, helping me out would have to include getting out of this bathroom stall. Quince is more than filling my personal space and I'm feeling uncharacteristically claustrophobic. The graffiti-covered walls are closing in. Sweat droplets form on my forehead.

"Let me out," I demand, ignoring his offer of help. "It stinks in here."

I give him a look that implies he is the source of the odor, even though he smells like leather and mint toothpaste. He doesn't get offended like a normal guy would. No, he flashes me that arrogant smile and leans closer. Just when I think he's going to press his entire body into mine, he scoots sideways, next to the toilet, and out of the way of the door.

Yanking the door open, I burst into the bathroom and take a deep breath of non-Quinced air.

"As I was saying," he continues when he follows me out of the stall, "I'm going to help you catch your big fish at the dance."

"But," I argue as the oxygen returns to my brain, "he doesn't want—"

"He doesn't know what he doesn't want."

Leaning back against the edge of the sink, I cross my arms over my chest and nod to show I'm listening. Though mostly I'm thinking about how relieved I am to be out of that stall and several feet away from Quince.

"To get Ben"—he clears his throat—"nett's attention,

you need to do something special. Surprising." He smiles. "Shocking."

"And what," I ask, skeptical, "do you suggest?"

He slips his hands into the back pockets of his jeans, stretching his T-shirt tight across his chest. From a purely objective standpoint, I admit it's a nicely formed chest. Probably sculpted from all those hours trying to keep his motorcycle running and his part-time job at the lumberyard. And he does have yummy dark blond hair and those great blue eyes that remind me of home. If he weren't such an obnoxious jerk, Quince might actually be an attractive guy.

"I'll tell you," he says, "in the parking lot after school."

Then, without any explanation, he spins on his biker boots and walks out of the bathroom. What the heck does that mean? I'm still frowning and trying to figure out what just happened—I was *not* admiring his chest!—when he sticks his head back in.

"Want to know why I thought Courtney's little tirade was so funny?"

I shrug, expecting him to say I'll find that out after school, too. If I meet him, that is. I don't expect him to answer.

But Quince is nothing if not unexpected.

"She bought me these boots."

He flashes me a quick smile, and then he's gone.

And I have the rest of the day to decide if I can risk accepting his offer of help. In three hours and— I lift my wrist to check the time.

Damselfish! I'm nearly fifteen minutes late to art. Shannen's probably worried about me. I take off down the hall, wondering if I'm actually going to meet Quince in the parking lot. Mrs. Ferraro probably hasn't even noticed I'm not there.

4

"*H*e did *what?*" Shannen shouts as she cuts out a picture of Brad Pitt to paste into her collage.

"Quiet," I snap. I don't need the entire art class knowing what happened in the bathroom. It's bad enough they already know what happened in the cafeteria.

Shannen lowers her voice to as close to a whisper as she can manage. "He trapped you in the *stall?*"

"Yes." Rescued is more like it, though I'm not about to admit that out loud.

I find a picture of a dolphin in *National Geographic* and quickly tear out the page. We are each making a "biographical collage" using magazines and catalogs. So far, I've got an underwater background, a pair of clown fish, and a Swarovski tiara from Neiman Marcus. Thankfully, Mrs. Ferraro is all about abstract expression. She won't question the weirdness in my collage, as long as I have a convincing reason.

"You know . . . ," Shannen murmurs, staring intently at her picture, "Quince kind of looks like Brad. Dark blond hair, square jaw line, piercing blue eyes. I wouldn't mind being stuck in a stall with him for an hour or two."

I refuse to even respond to that. Quince Fletcher is as far from Brad Pitt as a sea cucumber is from becoming king of Thalassinia.

"He always wears those tight biker tees, and his jeans are worn smooth in just the right spots—"

"Enough!" I stab some glue to the back of the dolphin picture and slap it down onto my collage. "We are not talking about *him*. All right?"

"All right," Shannen says slowly, tucking a lock of dark brown hair behind her ear. "Why did you glue that dolphin upside down?"

Okay, so I'm a little distracted. "He's doing the backstroke."

Shannen shrugs and goes back to her collage. I'm sure I haven't heard the last of it. She's not exactly the let-it-go type.

But my mind is less on Quince and more on his offer.

I haven't felt so conflicted since Daddy asked if I wanted to go live with Aunt Rachel for a while. At the time I'd known for only a few days about Mom being a terraped. All of a sudden there was this whole other side of me that I didn't even know about. Then Daddy told me Mom had a sister who lived on the mainland off the western edge of

our kingdom. Aunt Rachel knew all about us, about me, and when Daddy'd gone to talk to her about me learning the truth about Mom, she'd suggested I might like to go to high school. The same high school my mom had attended.

He asked me what I wanted to do, and I honestly didn't know the answer. Part of me really wanted to find out everything I could about Mom. She'd died long before I could remember, and the chance to learn more about her was really appealing. Another part of me was scared to death at the idea of moving into a completely foreign world. I'm a mermaid—*mer*, as in sea. I belong in the ocean.

In the end, curiosity overcame my fear.

My emotions are swirling just as wildly right now. On top of Quince's bizarre offer, I'm not exactly thinking clearly after the whole I-love-you-but thing.

I sigh as I cut out a picture of a girl with crazy blond hair.

"So," Shannen says after gluing tons of little pink hearts from a perfume ad around Brad's head, "are you going to meet him?"

"Meet who?" Since I am blocking Quince from my thoughts, I can't imagine who she's talking about. Or at least I'm trying to block him from my thoughts.

She spears me with a don't-play-games-with-me-I'm-your-best-friend-and-I-know-you-way-better-than-that look.

My shoulders slump. "I don't know."

"Let's consider your choices." She sets down her scissors and pushes her collage to the side so she can lean closer. "Option A: You do things your way, like you did at lunch, and end up with the same old results."

Wincing, I shake my head. I'll pass on a repeat of that moment, thank you very much. Clearly I can't catch Brody on my own.

"Right," she says. "Option B: You take a chance that Quince, who presumably has a Y chromosome in his DNA and happens to have insider information from your target's ex-girlfriend, can actually help you."

I run a hand through my hair. My fingers get stuck in the mess of curls, and I have to wiggle them free.

"That leaves me with two questions." I absently glue the clown fish so they are riding on the dolphin's belly. "One, will he actually help me, or is this just his latest trick to torment me? And two, if he actually does want to help . . . why?"

Shannen smiles wryly. "There's only one way to find out the answer to both of your questions."

Our eyes meet, my gaze resigned and hers matter-of-fact. We both say, "Meet him."

My stomach is so full of butterfly fish that I don't even laugh when Shannen says, "Jinx."

I'm putting my faith in Quince Fletcher.

I'm already jinxed.

* * *

In the fifteen minutes I spend waiting for Quince in the parking lot, my imagination desperately tries to come up with some idea of what his plan might possibly entail.

Maybe he's going to pay Brody to date me. Highly unlikely, since Quince and his mom have no money to spare. Maybe he's going to suggest *I* pay Brody to date me. Bad idea for so many reasons, not the least of which is the fact that I have even less money than Quince. You can't exactly get an after-school job with a Thalassinian Social Security number.

Ooh, maybe Quince is going to help me kidnap Brody and keep him tied up in our basement until he realizes he loves me. Unlikely. That idea has two major flaws. First, that only works in the old-timey romance novels Aunt Rachel reads. Second, we don't have a basement.

Okay, this waiting thing is getting ridiculous. I'm giving him to a count of twenty to show up, then I'm out of here.

Quince roars up on his motorcycle just when I've gotten to seventeen. I should have left after ten.

A plastic bag comes flying through the air and smacks me in the chest. Instinctively, I grab it before it falls. It feels soft and squishy.

Oh, no. It's rope and a hood, isn't it? He really is going to kidnap Brody. I take a deep breath and reign in my imagination. I scowl at Quince. If he hadn't kept me waiting so long, I never would have come up with these ridiculous ideas.

"What is this?" I ask, looking for a store label on the bag and only find THANK YOU FOR SHOPPING WITH US.

Quince grins. "Your costume."

"Excuse me?" I step off the curb and approach his bike warily. I've heard horror stories about parts flying off this piece of junk. "My costume?"

"For the dance." He grabs the bag back and opens it, pulling out a white frilly blouse and a multicolored, multiruffled skirt.

"A Spanish dancer?" I scoff, not really having anything against the idea other than it being Quince's.

He winks at me. "Nope," he explains. "A pirate wench."

"Wha—"

"I have it from a very reliable source," he continues, "that Bennett is going as a pirate. This is part one of two in Operation Surprise and Shock. Surprise him by going as his female counterpart." He holds up the costume. "A pirate wench for a pirate pans—"

"Fine!" I snatch the costume back. It could be worse. Shannen will approve, since it fits the Under the Sea theme. As I stuff it into my bag, I ask, "What if it doesn't fit?"

That arrogant smile returns. "Darlin'," he drawls, "I had you in my lap for a good ten minutes today. It'll fit."

I've been trying to block that memory from my mind all afternoon. Not that I succeeded. The scent of leather and mint toothpaste followed me everywhere. The scent of Quince.

My cheeks burn, but I am determined not to let him rattle me. "What is part two of the plan?"

"Mmm." He rubs his hands together. "Shock. This is the best part."

I don't think I'm going to like part two.

"At nine thirty, Brody is going to get a note asking him to meet Courtney in the library so she can give him back his class ring."

Oh, I know I'm not going to like part two.

"Only it won't be Courtney waiting for him. It will be you."

I hate part two.

"Then you kiss him. Shocking, no?"

No, I hate Quince. I love part two.

Not the kissing part—what kind of mergirl does he think I am?—but I can see the possibilities. Me and Brody. Alone. In the darkened library. Maybe I'll finally be able to find the courage to tell him how I feel. And maybe, if he shows even a hint of interest in return, I'll tell him even more. To Brody I would tell everything.

"I-I-I—" That's not coming out at all right. "How can I be sure it will—"

"Trust me." He kicks his motorcycle to life. "Just be in the library at nine thirty. I'll take care of the rest."

Then he mutters something I can't hear, but I catch the words "idiot" and "lesson." I'm so excited, I don't even care.

Lifting his boot from the pavement, Quince twists the gas and squeals out of the parking lot. My insides are a mess. All I can think of are the *what ifs*.

What if this is all a trick?

What if it's not?

What if Brody hates me?

What if he doesn't?

What if everything goes according to plan and I confess everything to Brody in the library tomorrow night at nine thirty?

That's the scariest *what if* of all.

Before I can go down that path, thinking about what that could mean for my future, for *our* future, Quince roars back into the parking lot and squeals to a stop in front of me. Why can't he ever just leave and stay gone like a normal person?

"By the way," he asks, keeping his eyes trained on mine, "do you always keep notes in your . . . *private* pocket?"

"In my—"

He flicks his gaze down to my chest and back to my eyes.

I gasp and clutch my book bag in front of me. In the morning's craziness I'd totally forgotten the message from Daddy.

"Perv!"

He just winks and then roars back out to the street. Was that a tint of blush I saw on his cheeks? Doubtful. Quince is never shy about anything. When he is out of sight and I can't hear the roar of his bike anymore, I drop my bag and reach into my bra.

As I begin the walk home, I break the royal seal and unfold the note.

FROM THE DESK OF

KING WHELK OF THALASSINIA

Dearest Lily,

*Your cousin Dosinia's sixteenth-birthday celebration
is this weekend. I'm sure she would love to have you attend.
Also, I miss you a great deal. Why don't you come home
for a few days?*

Yours,

Daddy

Not likely. I mean, I love Dosinia . . . mostly (she can be a little boy crazy and kind of a brat) and I totally love my dad. But hopefully, if everything works out tomorrow night, I'll be spending the weekend with the boy I love. No birthday party in all the seven seas could top that.

5

"*D*id you ask him?" Peri asks before I've even had a chance to transfigure in the shadowy waters beneath Seaview Pier.

When I left Thalassinia, we agreed to meet once a week between here and home. Since mer and human calendars don't quite match up, she swims to the coast to meet me on Thursday afternoon, the equivalent of Friday in the sea. She's my link to the ocean world when I don't have time to visit home—which I haven't done in almost three months.

Also, Peri knows me better than anyone. She's like my personal therapist.

Turning to the sound of her voice, I say, "Yes, I asked him."

"Congratu—"

"And he turned me down."

"Oh, honey," she says, swimming into view. "I'm so sorry."

At the sight of her super-sympathetic face—her mouth tightened into a sad shadow of a smile, her eyes soft and gentle—I break down all over again. The tears come back, vanishing into the salty sea, and I take only a tiny bit of solace in the thought that, in the shadows of the pier above, Peri won't be able to see my eyes glittering.

I allow myself a second to relive my pain at Brody's rejection. Just a brief moment when I let the pain course through me, reminding me of my foolish hope, before I push it to the back of my mind.

That's not what I need to talk to her about. The asking-Brody-to-the-dance thing is over, and now I have another reason to seek her advice.

"I don't want to talk about that," I say. "I need to talk about what came next."

She takes my hands in hers, giving me a reassuring squeeze. "Tell me everything."

And I do.

As we start to swim out to sea, leaving the human-dense shore for the safety of the barrier reef a few nautical miles out, I tell her every last pathetic detail about the paper-wad incident and finally asking Brody at lunch and my complete and total meltdown afterward and how Quince Fletcher—*Quince Fletcher,* of all people!—came to my aid. Peri knows my stormy history with the blowfish, so she's just as shocked as I was about his behavior.

"And then," I exclaim, stopping at the western edge of

the reef, "he offered to help! He has this plan where I'll wait in the library during the dance and he'll get Brody to go in there so I can kiss him."

"Kiss him?" Peri gasps. "You're not really going to kiss him, are you?"

"No, of course not," I reassure her. "I'm not stupid. But it will be dark, and I might have the courage to finally tell Brody how I feel about him."

Peri looks beyond relieved that I'm not going to kiss an unsuspecting and unwilling Brody. I may be a girl in love, but I'm not dishonest. I would never trick anyone into that.

"That sounds like a good plan," she says. "What's not to like?"

I don't ask how she knows I don't like it—after more than a dozen years of best friendship, she can practically read my mind.

"It's Quince," I explain. "I don't trust him."

"That's nothing new."

"I know." I run my hands through a small green clump of mermaid's-hair, letting the silky seaweed slip through my fingers. "But the problem is . . . I *want* to trust him this time."

Peri swims around behind me and starts absently braiding my hair. It feels nice, because on land my hair can't be coaxed into anything but a blond halo. And once I get back to Seaview, her braid will dry too tight for me to leave it in. Moments like these are my only reprieve from the frizz.

"So you're afraid," she says, "that, because he's offering to help with the one thing you want most, he might be setting you up for the biggest fall of all."

"Exactly!"

I hadn't put it into those words, but that's my fear.

She circles her fingertips over a spot just below my neck, and I know she's tracing my mer mark—the tattoolike design all merfolk are born with that brands them as a child of the sea. I picture the design, a circle of waves surrounding a stylized kelp flower, lime green to match my scales. Peri's, I know from experience, is copper. Daddy's is royal blue.

When a mermaid is in terraped form, the mark is the only thing that distinguishes her from a human.

"I don't see how." Finished with my braid, Peri swims around to face me. "All you'll be doing is waiting in a library, right?"

I nod.

"Then I don't see any way for him to make it anything other than what it is." She tilts her pretty brunette head to the side. Even when she's on land, her long, silky chestnut hair flows in elegant waves down her back, lucky mergirl. "Do you?"

"No." I shake my head slowly. "And that makes me nervous."

Because it wouldn't be the first time that Quince did something I hadn't even remotely anticipated. But she's right. At this point I don't really have anything to lose.

"I almost forgot," Peri squeals, taking my hand in hers. "I have something to show you."

She pulls me along the edge of the reef, down deeper near the seafloor where the sunlight above starts to fade. When we reach the sandy bottom, Peri tugs me to a small cave opening that looks like nothing more than an oversized crab hole. Without another word, she releases my hand and kicks into the hole. She disappears into the reef.

I'm not surprised. Peri loves to find secret spots, especially ones that are totally hidden from view.

Swimming after her, I duck into the hole and find myself in a very narrow tunnel. Good thing I'm not claustrophobic or, you know, afraid of drowning. After about ten feet, the tunnel opens onto a big cavern.

"Wow," I say with undisguised awe.

It's beautiful.

Even though the cavern is fully enclosed by reef, the entire space is full of light. I float up to the top. The ceiling is actually a paper-thin layer of coral that looks like solid reef from above, but still lets in plenty of sun. Just like a skylight.

"Check out the walls," Peri says, drawing my attention away from the nearly transparent ceiling.

I twist down, studying the side surfaces of the cavern. They are covered with a rainbow of starfish. Orange and red and yellow stars overlap to make a sunset-colored wallpaper on the coral walls.

"I totally want this on the walls in my room," I say.

Peri smiles, swimming over to the starfish-covered surface and running her fingertips over their prickly backs. "I thought you might like it."

Boy, do I miss her. Without our once-a-week meetings, I don't think I'd be making it through my time on land. Thankfully, that won't last forever.

"As soon as I get back," I say, trying to think positively about the future, "we'll decorate my bedroom in flames of starfish."

"Sounds like a plan," she replies. "Now you just need to hurry up and hook your terraped boy so you can come home." She sounds all teasing and jokey, but I know she's secretly serious.

She's missed me just as much as I've missed her.

"I promise," I tell her. And myself. I want to get back to life as planned, too.

Tomorrow night at the dance, I'm going to make it happen.

6

*A*unt Rachel manages to take what feels like two hundred thirty-eight pictures before I leave for the dance, and I think Prithi meowed her way into about two hundred thirty of them. I'm excited, too, but I think the first hundred captured every last detail for posterity.

"Your father will love these," she says, snapping a couple more.

Glancing at myself in the front hall mirror, I'm not so sure. After pulling on the skirt and blouse from Quince's bag-o'-costume-fun, I found some accessories in the bottom of the bag. Big gold hoop clip-on earrings. A red bandana headband. And a brown leather beltlike thingy that turned out to be more of a corsetlike thingy that laces up the front. If Daddy saw me like this, he'd strike his trident to the seafloor with enough force to start a minor tsunami, for sure. That whole idea that mermaids swim around topless?

Totally untrue. That's why we invented the bikini top.

I've untucked the blouse and tugged it up a few inches in order to pass Aunt Rachel's chaperone test. No way she's letting me out of the house with my cha-chas hiked up for the world to see.

"You look like a pirate princess," she says, setting down the camera and stepping closer. She gets that sad look in her eyes, and I know she's thinking about Mom again.

I never knew my mother, but I've seen pictures. I know I got my blond curls from her—although hers never looked frizzy. I know she was always smiling. Always at the beach or in the pool. And I know that, until three years ago, I thought she was a mermaid. When I found out she was human, it was like my entire world crashed against the shore. Imagine finding out at fourteen that you were adopted and your real parents were the king and queen of France. (I know France doesn't have a monarchy anymore, but this is a hypothetical imagining.) That's how amazed and startled and confused and excited I was.

Some merfolk hate terrapeds. They think humans are a plague upon the seas who should be banned from the waters they so often abuse. But not me. And not Daddy, obviously, since he fell in love with one. I'd always been a little intrigued by humans and their culture—how very *Little Mermaid* of me, I know—but when I found out I was half human, then my interest became more personal. The longer I live among them, the more connected I become. I don't even think of them as terrapeds (the mer term for humans) anymore. That connection I feel will never go away. I belong in the sea, but hanging out on land has its perks (aka Brody, Aunt Rachel, Shannen, and, you know, lip gloss). Plus, it makes me feel closer to Mom.

The look in Aunt Rachel's eyes now is the same look she had when I first showed up at her front door. Sorrowful joy.

"Thanks," I say quietly.

"With that makeup on, you look twenty-five." Her eyes, green like mine, fill with tears, but she smiles like she's trying to hide them. "You look just like your mother."

Before she can erupt into sobs, I wrap my arms around her and squeeze. Even though it makes her sad sometimes to have me around because I remind her of Mom, I think we're both glad to have a new way of connecting with her. For Aunt Rachel, I'm the living heritage of her sister. For me, my aunt is the scrapbook of Mom's life.

We stand there for a few minutes until I hear a horn outside.

"That's Shannen," I say, stepping back. "I have to go."

"Have fun tonight, Lily."

"I will," I say with a smile. "Tonight's going to be special, I just know it."

Her brow wrinkles into a concerned frown. "You're not going to do anything reckless, are you?" Her eyes search my face. "You have to be careful. You're not like other girls."

Don't I know it.

The horn sounds again.

"I promise." I say. "Nothing reckless." Although our definitions of reckless might not match up perfectly.

Before she can say more, I press a quick kiss to her cheek and dash out the door. "I'll check in when I get home."

Prithi meows in protest of my departure.

Honk, honk.

"Don't rush into anything," Aunt Rachel calls as I hop down the front steps.

Don't rush into anything? I laugh, hurrying down the sidewalk. I've been waiting three years for this night. That's taking it slow for a sea slug.

"Nice costume," Shannen calls out as I approach her car. Through the passenger window I can see she's dressed as— you guessed it—a mermaid. "Where'd you get it?"

"Actually, I—"

"From me."

My entire body tenses.

Speaking of sea slugs.

I should have known he wouldn't let a chance to humiliate me go by. I spin around in the direction of his voice. In the setting sunlight, I don't see him at first. Then he shifts and I see him leaning against his front porch, just a few feet away, that cocky, one-sided smile making him look like an arrogant blowfish. Which he is.

But Shannen and Peri and I all agreed that I should let him help me—whatever that means.

"Yes," I bite out. "From Quince."

"You make a pretty pirate wench, princess."

I open my mouth to retort, but then I realize . . . that might have been a compliment. At least the closest to one Quince has ever gotten.

The polite thing to do would be to thank him.

I turn and yank open the car door.

"You know," he says, his voice velvety soft, "you could go to the dance with me. Jealousy would grab Benson's attention."

I am so stunned by his suggestion that I don't even correct Brody's name. I am frozen, hand on the door handle. Then I feel warmth at my back, and I know he's standing right behind me.

My skin prickles.

Tonight he still smells of mint toothpaste, but instead of leather the other scent is something . . . earthy. Like Aunt Rachel's garden after a rain.

"Um, no," I stammer. "No thanks. I'll stick with the original plan."

I feel something brush the back of my neck.

"Your loss, princess," he whispers in my ear.

The warmth disappears, and I know he's gone. My body erupts in goose bumps at the sudden chill. Without turning to look, I open the door and slip into the passenger seat.

"Let's go." My voice sounds breathless.

When Shannen doesn't start the car right away, I look up. She is staring at me. Did something happen to my makeup? I've actually managed—with Aunt Rachel's help—to successfully apply some mascara. But maybe it smudged during pictures or something. I flip down the visor to do a spot check. Nope, everything still in place. Maybe she's just not used to seeing me with face paint—

"What," she asks, "was that?"

Oh. *That*. Since I don't know what *that* was, I can't exactly answer. I think Quince just enjoys toying with my sanity. He's pretty much beyond comprehension.

"Nothing," I assure her. "He just wanted to make me nervous."

She stares at me a few seconds longer before shrugging and pulling out into the street. She knows Quince defies explanation.

All the way to school, my insides quiver and churn like rough seas in a squall. I don't know if I'm going to make it through the night. Then, as we pull into the parking lot, I see Brody get out of his Camaro dressed—just like Quince told me—as a pirate. For the first time in three years, seeing him actually settles my nerves instead of agitating them.

That's when I know everything will be okay. Brody is my mermate, and tonight is the beginning of our future. Nothing is going to stand in my way.

7

*T*he library is dark and empty when I slip through the glass double doors at nine fifteen. I know I'm early, but I want a little time to calm down, to prepare myself. For the last hour, I've been dancing and talking with friends, trying to have a good time despite my looming appointment. In just fifteen minutes I'm going to confess my feelings to the boy I've been seriously in love with for what seems like forever.

A girl needs a little time to reflect.

For three years, I've watched Brody from afar. Loved him even as he looked right past me for the most part. Occasionally I wonder why, exactly, I love him so much. I mean, we've never even shared a meaningful conversation that didn't revolve around swimming or news team.

Maybe it's his charm. On my first day at Seaview I walked nervously through the cafeteria on wobbly land legs without a soul to sit with. As I scanned the unfamiliar setting, searching for an empty place to eat, I lost my balance and tumbled, tray of enchiladas first, into Brody's lap. Instead of freaking out or yelling or humiliating me (like *some* boys), he laughed and helped me clean up the mess. He's one of those guys who can make everyone—even an awkward mermaid on her first day of human school—feel special.

Or maybe it's how he seems to be comfortable in any situation. No matter where he is at the moment, Brody always belongs, and for a human transitioning to the mer world, I think that must be a key character trait.

And the fact that he's so at home in the water is a major bonus in the potential mermate category.

Whatever the reason, my heart flutters every time I see him, and I can't deny that. I don't want to. My body and my heart know things my brain doesn't necessarily understand.

The fifteen minutes race by. Before I know it, I'm staring at the clock as it ticks past nine thirty. Nine thirty-five. Nine forty.

At nine forty-five I decide he's not coming. Rather than freak out, I try to rationalize. Maybe that's a good thing. After all, he thought he was meeting Courtney. Clearly he doesn't even want to see her long enough to get his ring back. That must mean he's totally over her. Right?

Then, just as I'm buying into my argument, a shadow

appears in the doorway.

My heart slams once against my chest, freezes for a good ten seconds, then starts beating faster than ever.

He's here. He's actually here.

I don't care if he's here to meet Courtney—he's here and I'm about to take the biggest chance of my life.

In the dim light from the hall I can make out the red bandana tied over his head. I watch, in awe, as he walks through the library, weaving through the sea of tables, heading directly for my hidden corner. He moves like a deep sea current—smooth and powerful. It's like I'm watching him walk for the first time.

Then he's right in front of me.

I can only make out his outline, but I get the feeling he's looking directly into my eyes.

Tell him! That's why you're here. Open your mouth, form the words, and—

His hand cups the back of my neck, and before I can think, he dips down and our mouths meet. For a split second I worry that he thinks he's kissing Courtney. But the instant the warmth of his soft lips spreads into mine, all thoughts dissolve. Pure feeling is all I have left. Little electric sparks zip through my bloodstream, making sure every nerve in my body is focused on his amazing mouth.

Instinct takes over, and I lift my arms to wrap around his neck, pulling him closer. My fingers brush against his cheek, feeling the rough stubble of an unshaven face. An uncontrolled growl bursts from deep inside me, and I pull him even closer.

He tilts to the side a little, opens his mouth, licks his tongue across my lips, and then—

Pulls back.

My mind whirls. My lungs struggle for oxygen. I feel myself start to transfigure, my body reacting as if I am in water and need my gills. Shaking my head, I regain a little control and stop the change.

My emotions, too, are going insane. Not only do I feel my own raging joy and passion, but because of the new connection we just forged, I can feel some of his, too.

"Wow," I gasp. "That was . . ."

I can't find the words.

He can. "Incredible."

My eyes pop open and I am instantly alert. That didn't sound like Brody's voice. That sounded more like—

"Bet Benson could never kiss you like that."

"How was your night, dear?" Aunt Rachel asks when I stomp into the house.

"Fine," I snap, slamming the front door behind me. "Just perfect."

I ignore the muffled *"Ow!"* followed by loud banging.

"Lily," he shouts, "let me in."

Aunt Rachel looks at me. "Is something wrong?"

"No," I answer sweetly, "of course not."

Bang, bang. "Let me explain."

"Is that Quince?"

"I wouldn't know," I say, and start up the stairs to my bedroom.

Bang, bang. "I never planned to kiss you."

I freeze, one foot hovering above the next step, my heart hammering in my chest. I can feel Aunt Rachel's sharp gaze focus on me.

"Oh, Lily," she gasps, "you didn't."

I whip around. "No," I blurt out, tears floating just below the surface, "*I* didn't." I stomp down the stairs, walk to the door, and fling it open. One finger, shaking with fury, points at the pirate-clad nightmare standing on our front stoop. "*He* did!"

The nightmare, apparently thinking my opening the door is an invitation, takes a step forward. I slam the door harder.

"*Ow!*"

I hope his nose is broken.

"Wiwy," he says in a voice that sounds like he's squeezing his nose—victory! "Just wet me expwain—"

I throw the dead bolt.

"I'll be in my room," I announce, and head for the stairs again.

"Oh, no, you don't," Aunt Rachel says, grabbing me by the arm as I go by. "You have some explaining to do yourself, girl."

For a second I am a rock, utterly unemotional and ready to tell Aunt Rachel to leave me alone. The next, all the emotion and craziness of the last half hour—from the moment I kneed Quince in the squids until I slammed the door in his face for the second time—just bubbles up to the surface, and I explode.

I whirl around to face her. "It was going to be perfect. I was going to tell Brody how much I love him, and he was going to realize how perfect we are for each other, and we were going to begin our life together." I swallow over the lump in my throat. "Perfect."

"My sweet, innocent girl," Aunt Rachel whispers, gently wiping a tear off my cheek. She shakes her head like she's disappointed in me—which is completely unfair since I'm not the one who caused this mess. I'm totally the victim in this situation.

"Perfect," I repeat with a snap, startling the sad look off her face. "Until *he* messed it up. *He* showed up instead of Brody. *He* kissed me and made my fins curl. *He*"—I shout loud enough to be heard through the door—"ruined my entire life."

Then, before Aunt Rachel can say whatever is behind the shocked look in her eyes, I yank my arm free and run for my room.

That's it, I'm done with this human thing. I'm going back to the sea. Where I belong. Human life is too complicated, and humans—one human in particular—are not to be trusted. (Except for Aunt Rachel, of course. And Shannen. And Brody. And maybe my art teacher.) I don't know what made me ever think I could handle this world.

Dropping to my knees, I peer behind the grass bed skirt in search of a bag to pack my things. No bag. Then I jump up, hitting my head on my nightstand, sending my palm-tree lamp crashing to the floor, and startling Prithi from her nap on my stuffed animal–covered bed. Whatever. I don't need a bag. I don't have anything to take.

Sure, my room is full of random stuff I've collected over the past three years, but I won't need any of it in Thalassinia. Water is rough on land-produced objects. Besides, all I want to do is forget the human world ever existed.

Well, everything but Brody—

"Lily."

What is he doing here?

Aunt Rachel. She must have let him in to—

The doorknob starts to turn, but I dive for it and twist the lock just in time.

"Lily," he repeats. His voice sounds disappointingly broken-nose-free. "Please, just let me explain what happened."

"No." I grab a stuffed dolphin from my bed, sending Prithi leaping to the ground, and fling it at my door. It barely makes a soft *thud* before tumbling to the floor, but I feel better. "Go away."

Meow.

"I really planned to help you snag Ben"—he clears his throat—"nett." His voice drops to a mumble. "Figured if you spent more than ten minutes with him, you'd realize he's a total pr—"

"I'm not listening to you," I shout. And fling a stuffed Shamu against the door. And a stuffed lobster. And a stuffed sea horse.

Prithi, thinking it's a game, bounds after my artillery. She takes possession of the sea horse and retreats under my bed.

"What I mean is, I gave him the note. He was supposed to be there." He clears his throat again. "Then I"—*ah-hem*—"saw him dancing with"—*ah-hem*—"Kiran Siman"—*ah-hem*—"and I thought I should"—*ah-hem*—"check on you. Damn, my throat is dry."

He breaks into a fit of throat clearing that soon turns into coughing.

Great. Dry throat. I squeeze my eyes shut but can't make it go away. The change is happening already.

"Anyway," he says when he's through coughing for the moment, "you looked so . . . expectant standing there in the dark." His voice sounds sad, but maybe that's just the change, too. "Like you were waiting for the best moment of your life."

Cough, cough, cough.

I look at the sad pile of stuffed sea creatures clustered around my door. He's right, of course. I was waiting for the most perfect moment of my life.

Then he ruined it.

I fling another round of stuffed sea life at the door. "I wasn't"—starfish—"waiting"—great white shark—"for *you*."

My bed is now empty of stuffed animals. I'm about to grab a pillow when I hear a *plunk* against the door from the outside. It sounds like a forehead smacking against the wood.

"I know," he groans. He coughs a few times before adding, "I couldn't help it."

There is such a sound of despair in his voice that when he starts coughing again, I find myself pressing a hand to the door, as if that will heal him. Only I know it won't, because he's not sick. He's changing. And I can't just run away from this. Or from him.

Even Prithi ventures out and meows softly at the door.

"Water," I say quietly.

There is a long, silent pause before he asks, "What?"

"Water," I repeat. "You need a drink of water."

"It's just a cough," he insists. "Lily, I want you to understand why I—"

"Go ask Aunt Rachel for a glass of water."

"I'm right here, dear," Aunt Rachel offers.

Great, a witness to my humiliation.

"Listen to me, please," he asks, his voice raspy like sandpaper.

If he doesn't drink some water soon—a *lot* of water—he'll lose it altogether. Not that I'm interested in listening to him, but some little part of me does want to know why *he*, the guy who lives for my torment, kissed me.

"Aunt Rachel," I say, ignoring his plea, "get Quince a glass of water."

"Of course," she says, and from the take-charge tone, I can tell she knows this is serious.

I sigh. "And make it salty."

"Right," she says. Then I hear her walking down the stairs.

"Salty?" Quince asks. "Why the hell would I drink salt water?"

"It's a long story."

Prithi meows sympathetically.

A heavy pause hangs between us. "Why do I think," he says, "when you say that, it's a gross understatement?"

"Listen," I say, leaning my forehead against the door. "Drink the water. Go home and take a bath. A *salt* bath. You'll feel better—"

"No," he argues. "I'm not leaving until you let me expl—"

He breaks into a huge coughing fit before he can finish.

"I'm not up for this right now," I say, and I can hear the weariness in my voice. This has been an emotional day, and he's lucky I'm not prepared to fillet him alive at the moment.

"Okay," he says quietly. "As long as you promise we'll talk tomorrow."

Oh, we'll talk tomorrow. When he pressed his lips to

mine, he got way more than he bargained for. It may not be anything he wants to hear, but we'll talk. Because in order to undo what he started, I have to present him before the royal court of Thalassinia. Aka my dad.

"I promise." When he starts coughing again, I add, "Just go home and take a bath."

How did I ever get myself into this mess?

And how am I ever going to get myself out?

Looks like I'm going home for the weekend after all.

*M*eet me at Seaview Beach Park at three.

I slipped the note under Quince's front door first thing in the morning and then disappeared. A night's lack of sleep hadn't cleared things up for me, and I needed a full day to figure out how to explain . . . well, *everything* . . . to him.

As the sun heads west behind me, I sit staring out at the ocean horizon. Still not sure how I'm going to proceed.

How do you tell a guy you're a mermaid? And that he's turning mer, too? I've spent three years fantasizing about telling Brody, but this is different. Quince is different.

He doesn't say anything when he walks up behind me, but I feel him. In the sand, in the air. Everywhere. For a minute, I let the tension—or maybe it's the bond, I still can't believe I'm bonded to Quince Fletcher—crackle between us. I'd always heard the bond was an addictive high. I never expected the kind of physical connection I'm feeling.

I wonder if he feels it, too.

"Do you believe in other worlds?" I finally ask.

"What?" He laughs softly. "You mean like alien planets?"

"No, worlds right here on Earth," I explain. "Worlds you can't see. Worlds you never knew existed but that were there all the time."

He drops down onto the sand next to me, arms hanging over his bent knees. "What's this all about, princess?"

A wave crashes in front of us. Princess. That almost makes me smile. And cry.

"Look at the sand." I point to the area at our feet. "See all those shells?"

"Yeah. . . ."

"Those are coquinas."

"Right, they come in on the waves—"

"That's what everyone thinks." I shake my head. "Look closer."

A wave crashes, leaving behind a rainbow array of coquinas. As we watch, they quickly wiggle back under the sand.

"Whoa!" Quince leans forward and scoops up a handful of sand. He inspects his scoop like a little boy digging for sea slugs beneath the ocean floor.

"They don't come in on the waves," I explain. "They live under the sand."

A softer wave rolls in, this one too gentle to displace the sand above the buried coquinas.

"Look at the water." The sea flows back out. "See all the ripples?"

Quince looks up from his handful of sand and stares at the ebbing tide.

"The coquinas cause the ripples." Another wave crashes, uncovering the rainbow of shells. "Even though they are hidden, they still affect the visible world."

"Wow," Quince says, his voice full of awe. "That's amazing."

"An entire world, hidden, but causing ripples in the world you know. The world you see."

Without turning to look, I can tell Quince is staring at the sand as if it's just come to life. Which it pretty much has. This is a good sign, I think. At least he wasn't, like, "whatever" or "so what." That has to bode well for my revelation. Right? I hope.

"That," I say, swallowing over my hesitation, "is kind of what Thalassinia is like."

He twists around to look at me. "Thala-what?"

"Thalassinia." I turn away from the sea to meet his gaze. "My kingdom."

To his credit, he blinks only three times before recovering his ability to speak.

"Your kingdom?" he echoes. "What exactly do you—"

"I'm not your average high school girl." I meet his confused look without flinching. "I'm a . . ." Now that the moment has finally come for me to tell someone the truth about who and what I am, it's a lot tougher than I thought.

Secrecy is paramount in the mer world. Besides the whole flee-at-the-first-sign-of-humans instinct, we also keep our world carefully camouflaged. With a few exceptions—like the Bimini Road and those underwater temples off the coast of Japan—our buildings look like naturally forming phenomena. We even have the ability, in extreme cases, to alter the memory of an untrustworthy human who has seen our world. It's not a fun experience, but it's a price worth paying to keep Thalassinia and the other mer kingdoms safely secret. If humans knew we really existed, if they believed we were something more than mystical creatures of ancient myth, we'd be in for a world of trouble. Scientists. Journalists. Government agencies with the ability to make entire kingdoms disappear. They'd all be knocking at our door— or, rather, swimming in our pool—in a flash. Our quiet world would become a maelstrom, and the peace we've spent centuries cultivating would vanish. Not exactly every mermaid's dream.

Every instinct and mer law I've been taught since birth commands me to keep our secret from humans at any expense, but I don't really have a choice. That kiss made this moment inevitable.

If this were Brody, it would be so much easier. I've been waiting for three long years to tell him the truth. But Quince? I'm not exactly prepared.

His eyebrows pinch together. He looks like he's thinking

really, really hard. And things are starting to connect in his brain.

"You know," he says, sounding skeptical, "that salty bath made me feel a world of better last night."

"It did?"

"And drinking the saltwater didn't dry me out. In fact"—his eyes narrow—"it made me feel superhydrated."

Ah-hem. "Good."

Why do I have the feeling I'm not going to have to figure out how to tell him anything? Maybe the bond is already giving us both some insights.

"Come to think of it," he adds, "you seem to take long baths pretty regularly."

"Hey," I shout, momentarily offended out of my anxiety by embarrassment. "You are such a peeping perv—"

"Lily"—his voice drops to an unusually serious level—"was there something more you wanted to tell me?"

"Well, actually," I reply, unable to look him in the eye any longer, "there was one thing. . . ."

When I don't finish, he says, "And that would be . . . ?"

I drop my head and mumble into my chest. For the love of Poseidon, this is harder than I ever imagined.

"What was that?" he asks, cupping my chin and forcing me to meet his questioning gaze. "I didn't quite catch it, since you were speaking at the sand."

"I said"—I twist out of his grasp and face him with as much fake boldness as I can muster—"I'm a mermaid."

His mouth drops open a little. I find myself staring at his lips, the same ones that were kissing me just last night. They are quite nicely formed. I never bothered to look before— since they were usually engaged in finding ways to mortify me—but they are nice and full, without being too soft. Kind of, as Shannen said, Brad Pitt–like. No wonder they felt so good—

Holy crab cakes, what's wrong with me? Why am I suddenly fanta—No. No, no, no. I am *not* fantasizing about my archenemy's lips! I must be totally losing it. I have way more pressing matters to deal with at the moment.

"Huh," Quince says, like he just saw a monkey riding a dolphin or something. Then he laughs. "That explains your bizarre obsession with fish terminology."

More laughter. I scowl. There's nothing amusing about this situation.

"Well, that's not half of it, buster." I slam my palms against his chest, sending him toppling back onto the sand. "You're turning into one, too."

He starts laughing even harder.

"What's so funny?"

"Aw, hell, Lil," he says. "Irony's a bitch."

I scowl harder. He is such a lunatic. Maybe I should just leave him here to dehydrate—

"I can't even swim."

Great. I jab both hands into my hair and hang my head.

Why am I surprised? Nothing about Quince has ever made my life easy. Thalassinia is forty-five nautical miles due east, and the blowfish can't swim. The sun is already closing in on the western horizon. There's no time to waste.

"Well, you're going to have to learn," I say, leaping to my feet. "And fast."

"Hold on there, princess." He stops laughing long enough to stand up. "Water and I are not exactly friends. I prefer transportation with wheels."

"That doesn't matter right now," I say, walking down to the ocean's edge and kicking off my shoes.

"The hell it doesn't," he growls.

"Listen." I turn to face him, hands on my hips. "We're working on a tight time schedule here. We don't want to be caught in open sea after dark."

When the sun goes down, the ocean turns into a war zone. All the biggest and baddest come out, and some of them have a taste for mermaid. Swimming the night sea without a guarded escort is shark-bait suicide.

He crosses his arms across his chest. "What exactly is going on?"

I can see I'm getting nowhere with him until I explain a few things. "When you kissed me last night, a bond formed and you began to turn mer. Your body started preparing itself for saltwater immersion, raising the saline levels in your skin to compensate—that's why the salty bath felt so good. Salivary glands near the top of your throat grew into gills so you'll be able to breathe underwater."

"Wait a second——"

"The chemistry of your lymphatic system is changing so it can regulate your buoyancy." I try not to laugh at the thought of Quince floating along on the surface as I drag his sorry self all the way to Thalassinia.

"My buoyancy was just fine——"

"Oh, and the bond?" I add before things go from bad to beyond repair. "Is this kind of chemical-hormonal-emotional connection thing that can kind of muddy your feelings. So don't go getting all mushy on me. We're not really falling for each other, even if we start to think we are."

Good advice for me, too.

I can't even imagine anything worse than thinking I'm in love with Quince. I'd be too embarrassed to ever leave the sea again.

"Okay . . . ," he says. "But what about——"

"No time," I interrupt once more—it feels good to finally be the one getting the last word. "I can dish more details later. First, I have to get you to the Thalassinian royal court so the king can perform the separation ritual, like, last week. Now get moving."

He looks stunned. Completely stunned. I never thought I'd see the day *I* shocked Quince Fletcher. And now that it's here, I don't have time to enjoy it. I've got to get this bond undone before the emotional stuff starts clouding my judgment, before his mer mark begins to form at the start of the next lunar cycle and the process becomes irreversible. *Ticktock, ticktock.*

"Let me get this straight," he says, recovering himself. "I'm turning into a mermaid because I kissed you?"

"I don't remember asking you to kiss me," I retort.

He scowls and I regret my snide remark. He didn't ask for any of this to happen, either. There was no way he could have known what he was getting himself into.

"Technically," I explain, "you're turning into a mer*man*."

He gives me a look that makes it clear that he's not interested in *technicalities* at the moment.

"Look," I say. "Can we just forget the last few days and focus on what we need to do right now?"

He shrugs, still sulking, from the look of his scowl. But we don't have time to indulge his pout. Unencumbered, I can make the swim from Seaview to Thalassinia in under two hours. With biker boy slowing me down, we'll be lucky to coast in before the suns sets in a few short hours.

"We don't want to be traveling when the sun goes down. I thought we would have more than enough time to spare, but I didn't know you couldn't swim." I turn and head again for the sea, unbuttoning my shorts as I go. "Follow me."

When I reach waist-deep water, I slip off my shorts and fling them back onto the beach next to my shoes. Next to a gaping Quince, who hasn't moved from the spot.

"Get your butt moving," I shout.

Jerking to a start, Quince finally starts walking. And reaching for the waistband of his cargo pants.

"*Uh-uh*," I call out. "You can keep your drawers on."

"But you—"

"I will be transfiguring," I explain. "Changing into my fins. You're not fully mer yet. You will be able to breathe and communicate underwater, but you won't transfigure into a merman."

And once the separation ritual is complete, he never will.

"Oh," he says, eyes slightly glazed and not sounding as if he understands at all.

There will be plenty of time later for Q and A.

"Lose the shirt, though," I order. "It'll only add drag and slow us down."

Without argument, Quince reaches for the hem of his Miami Ink tee and lifts it over his head. His skin gleams in the warm sunlight as he throws the shirt aside, landing right on top of my shorts. Lord love a lobster, he has a beautiful chest. He's not bodybuilder muscular, but clearly he's built enough to lift whatever comes along. I can just imagine him earning those muscles in the lumberyard, hefting plywood and two-by-fours to sculpt perfect pecs and a washboard—

"See something you like?"

My eyes jerk up. Caught staring at the off-limits eye candy. From the smoldering look in his eyes, he's not about to punish me. I shake my head slowly, unconvincingly. It's the bond. It has to be the bond. What else would—

He takes a step closer.

"No!" I squeak. "We have to, *um*, get going."

He stops and has the nerve to laugh.

The bond is already tweaking my thoughts. If I don't get us out of here and on the way to a full separation soon, I'm going to be in big—okay, *bigger*—trouble.

Quickly slipping my undies off, I throw them up to join my shorts and shoes on the beach. All I'm wearing is my tank top, which is all I'll need once I transfigure.

Quince stares at the water right in front of me, as if hoping to be able to see beneath the surface despite the distortion.

"Eyes up, buster."

In a slow, languid movement his eyes travel up over my wet top—hovering just a little on my cha-chas—and finally up to meet my angry gaze.

I feel my cheeks burn red.

"If we had time," I warn, "I would so punish you for that."

"You don't scare me, Princess," he replies with a grin.

Deciding that ignoring his comment is the best course of action, I ask, "Would you go lock our stuff in your bike?" The last thing I want is to come back later to find my clothes gone and have to ride all the way home in a finkini. (Manifesting a partial-transfiguration bikini bottom may be great for day-to-day modesty purposes, but straddling a motorcycle would be hard enough for me in regular shorts—I'm not about to attempt it with my backside covered in slippery scales.) Usually I bury my things in the sand beneath the pier, but I'd rather not traipse across the beach in the near-buff in front of Quince.

He lifts a brow.

"You *do* have a way to lock up stuff in your bike, don't you?" I taunt.

He looks like he wants to make another smart comment, but then he just shrugs and takes our pile up to the parking lot. He returns a few seconds later, slipping his keys into a Velcro pocket in his pants. That should hold them securely.

Time to get back to work. "The first step is aquarespire," I say as he approaches me in the surf.

"And that is . . . ?"

"Breathing water."

His dark blond brows furrow over stormy blue eyes. He's skeptical. Who wouldn't be? It's not like breathing liquid is a normal, everyday thing for humans. In fact, it's so abnormal that their brains usually make them do just about anything to keep from inhaling water, even fighting to the death. Literally.

"Follow me." I sink under the waves, letting my fins appear, lime green and gold scales covering my body from the waist down. My gills fill my throat, and I take a deep breath.

Quince doesn't follow.

I pop back above water. "What's wrong?"

"Kiss me."

"What?!?"

That's what got us into this mess in the first place.

"Kiss me," he repeats, stepping closer. "I trust you, but what do I know? If this is going to be my last breath, I want it to be a good one."

Then, before I can react or argue or escape, he slips an arm around my waist, yanks me closer, and presses his mouth to mine. Instinctively, my arms wrap around his neck, holding on for everything I'm worth. It's just like last night's kiss, only this time I know who I'm kissing. And this time the bond magnifies my every emotion. I can't think of anything but his lips moving over mine, of staying in his arms forever.

Thankfully, he's not so consumed by the bond. He's probably more experienced than me in the love department. It would be hard *not* to be more experienced than me, right?

He pulls back, leaving me breathing heavily.

"Okay," he says, his voice a little raspy. "I'm ready to go."

As he slips below the surface, I recover enough to say, "The first breath is the hardest."

9

"*Y*ou have to breathe."

Quince shakes his head, mouth clamped shut.

"If you don't," I argue, "you'll die."

He shrugs. As if he'd rather die than breathe water. Well, I'm not about to let him croak before we separate. I've heard stories about merfolk who've lost their bonded mates. They feel the connection forever, knowing they will never see their mates again. Without magical intervention, eventually some go mad.

I'm not about to go mad over Quince Fletcher.

He starts to push back to the surface. Before he can react, I dart behind him and wrap my arms around his stomach.

"I'm sorry," I say, "but this is the only way."

Then, before he can fight, I squeeze with every ounce of my strength. The last bit of air whooshes from his lungs, bubbling up to the surface above. He starts to struggle, twisting around and trying to yank my arms away. I squeeze tighter.

He goes limp. For half a second I think he's passed out.

"Breathe," I order, relaxing my hold a little so I can swim around to his front.

His eyes are wide open. Trying to take advantage of my slack grip, he pushes off the bottom and lunges for the surface. At the last moment I dive over him, forcing him down to the sandy bottom on his back.

"I know this is hard," I say, though I don't really know. I've always been able to breathe water.

But I can imagine it's pretty tough on the brain.

I stare directly into his eyes. "Trust me."

He blinks once and then nods slowly.

I watch as he opens his mouth, hesitates for a second, and then draws in a lungful of ocean. A look of uncertainty crosses his face as the water passes over his new gills for the first time. He holds the breath for a second and then releases. Then takes another. And another.

"Perfect," I say, smiling. "You're breathing like a pro."

He smiles back, a boy-am-I-happy-to-be-alive smile. His mouth moves like he's trying to say something.

"Oh, I forgot about that," I say. "We can't just talk like normal underwater."

He looks confused. And tries to speak again.

"Sound doesn't carry as well through gills. You have to

use a different level of your vocal cords." I point to the spot just above his Adam's apple. "Higher."

He just stares at me, looking confused—but breathing like he was born to it.

"Pretend you're talking like a girl."

No way, he mouths, shaking his head.

Stupid male ego.

"You won't *sound* like a girl," I assure him. "Because sound travels slower, the register of everything shifts lower. Just raise your pitch—"

"Like this?" he says, in a super-squeaky voice.

"Maybe a little lower," I suggest.

"Here?" he asks, sounding like his normal self.

I grin. "Perfect."

For a second I wonder how this whole thing would have gone—correction, *will* go—with Brody. As soon as I explain this whole mess to Daddy and we get our separation, I'm going back and confessing everything to Brody. And you can bet I won't hesitate this time. He's still my true love.

I bet he doesn't argue nearly so much.

"You know," Quince says, that dreaded honey in his voice, "you are in quite a compromising position."

That's when I realize I'm still lying over him, holding him against the sand so he can't escape to the surface.

I feel his hand curl around my waist and down over my—

With a swift flick of my fins, I shoot out of his grasp.

"Uh-uh, buster." I laugh. "No more funny business. We need to get to Thalassinia immediately."

"Okay," he says, rising to a sitting position. He does seem to be taking this really well. "How do we get there?"

I twist around onto my stomach and motion to my lower back. "Grab on."

"You've got to be—"

"I can travel over twenty nautical miles an hour." Almost as fast as a dolphin at full speed. "How about you?"

He grumbles something about being in the driver's seat but grabs me by either side of my waist.

"Hold on tight," I instruct. "And try to stay as stream-lined as possible."

I'm not used to swimming with human-sized drag on my back. He will probably cut my speed in half. Which means we're barely going to make it home before dark.

With a solid kick I set off to the east, heading toward the Bahamas. Now I have forty-five nautical miles of swimming time to worry about what Daddy's going to say when he sees my passenger.

I'm pretty sure it won't be "Welcome to the family."

To the untrained (human) eye, Thalassinia looks like an expanse of coral reefs and volcanic formations. There are no straight lines or geometric shapes to give away the fact that the structures are actually mermade. (Get it? Mer-made. Like mermaid, but . . . oh, never mind.) Thankfully, our kingdom is old enough for coral and algae and sea fans to have grown over all our buildings, camouflaging them even more from human eyes. Add on the strategically placed starfish, sea urchins, and anemones, and we're practically invisible.

Unless you know what to look for.

There is a rhythmic pattern to the organic shapes. The bioluminescent glow that illuminates the kingdom at night can be seen from a thousand yards away. And if you focus your attention on the largest formation at the center of the valley, you can make out the pattern of the Thalassinian flag, formed by a field of blue sea whips and green sponge seaweed covering the royal palace. My home.

As much as I'm dreading the meeting with Daddy—I can already hear him roaring, "What were you thinking?"—I can't help but be excited to be home. I haven't visited since winter break. Almost three months. Too, too long for a daughter of the sea.

"There it is," I say, pulling up as we crest the hill over-looking the valley. "That's Thalassinia."

Quince releases my waist and floats around to my side. I ignore the chill that shivers through me at the loss of his body heat: the depths are cool, that's all. I swirl my hands, spreading energy into the water around us to raise the temperature.

Before today, in the three years since we became neigh-bors, I've never once seen anything resembling shock on

Quince's face. He's more the shock-*inducing* type. But as he looks out on my kingdom for the first time, his jaw slacks and his eyes widen with a well-deserved sense of awe.

If this weren't the crappiest situation in the history of merkind, I would take some kind of perverse joy in rendering him speechless.

"Let's go," I say, swimming in front of him so he can grab on. "The sooner we get down there, the sooner I can get rid of you."

"Why, princess," he says as he slips strong arms around my waist, "I'm starting to get the impression you don't like me very much."

"You're only just figuring this out now?" I mutter as I kick us into motion.

I think he's going to fall back into the silence I enjoyed on the way over, until he says, "It must have been nice."

"What?"

"Growing up here," he says. "It must have been nice."

I never really thought about that. It wasn't like I had a choice of where to grow up. Or, at least, I didn't *think* I had a choice. But, yeah, I guess it was nice in a lot of ways. The sea is my home, and I'm always awed by her beauty. And I adore my dad more than anything, but my childhood wasn't always ideal. My dad wasn't just my dad; he was also the king. Growing up as the king's only daughter—only child, only heir—meant being protected and sheltered and practically held prisoner . . . in my own best interest, of course.

It meant being pressured from the time I could swim to act like a perfect princess, to find my mermate and bond before I turned eighteen or lose my place in the succession, while Daddy scared away every boy within ten kingdoms, insisting none were good enough for his baby girl. I love my dad and my kingdom and my royal future, but there were times when I just wanted to swim away and never look back.

Maybe that's why I jumped at the chance to go live with Aunt Rachel for a while. That's probably why Daddy suggested I go, giving me taste of freedom before I left to look for it on my own.

"You okay, princess?"

I almost forgot about the pain in the fins on my back.

"I'm fine," I snap. "Just trying to remember the way."

He doesn't need to know that mermaids have an innate navigational sense, kind of like butterflies. I could find my way home blindfolded if you dropped me off a random boat in the middle of the open sea.

Entering from the top edge of the kingdom—the Gulf Stream pushed us a little farther north than I planned—I swim over the outer suburbs, the cookie-cutter neighborhoods of identical coral homes with perfectly manicured caulerpa lawns, ring sets in the backyard, and a family seahorse in the garage. After the suburbs we pass over the commercial and industrial areas. I resist the urge to look in on my favorite shop, Bubbles and Baubles—they sell the most adorable shell jewelry and yummy all-natural soaps. I can go there anytime. *After* the separation.

Closer to the center are the older, more established neighborhoods. Many of the residents of the inner circle work in the palace. Peri's family lives there, just outside the royal complex, in a three-story home with a ship's bell on top. Her bedroom is on the top floor, and her window faces mine across the palace yard. We used to send bubble messages to each other long after we were supposed to be asleep.

When Quince and I reach the edge of the royal complex, I slow down. My heart rate kicks up to shark-attack pace. I'm almost as nervous to tell Daddy what happened as I was to ask Brody to the dance. Almost.

"This your place?" Quince asks. "Pretty fancy digs."

The royal complex is impressive.

It's supposed to be.

A low reef fence surrounds the grounds—it's more of a marker than a barrier, since anyone could just swim right over. Thalassinia and the other mer kingdoms have been at peace for years, and Daddy has an open-palace policy, so there's no reason to keep folks out.

The main gate—a pair of coral towers covered with sea whips and sponge seaweed—marks the end of the Great Thalassinian Way. Humans know this as the Bimini Road. Treasure hunters and myth seekers think it might be the remains of Atlantis. Nope, it's actually a really obnoxious "royal aisle." My great-great-great-great-grandfather had kind of an ego thing and wanted to force every merperson in the sea to swim a nautical mile to reach his throne. Even his guards. Which explains how he got devoured by a giant squid while they were still half a nautical mile away. Thankfully, our leadership abilities have improved since then.

Beyond the gate are the royal gardens, a vast seascape of rainbow-colored algae, kelps, corals, sponges, sea fans, and anemones. My tower room overlooks the gardens, and I used to love watching how they changed throughout the seasons. It's spring right now, so there are bright highlights of pink and yellow among the constant blues, greens, and browns. You can't help but feel the energy of spring with a field of magenta anemone petals below your window.

At the center of it all is the palace, a massive, vaguely star-shaped volcanic formation with five coral towers at the points. Out of habit I glance up at my window in the southwest tower. I'm surprised to find the light on. The cleaning staff is probably working late. Daddy always keeps my room ready, just in case I decide to pop home.

"By the way," I say as we approach the gates. "There's something you need to know before we go in."

As much as I'd like to keep my royal title a secret, I'm not going to get through this without Quince finding out the truth. Maybe if I tell him first, he'll keep his trap shut when we get inside.

"What's that, princess?"

"I'm not just any mermaid," I explain. "I'm a—"

"Princess Waterlily!"

I swallow a groan as one of the guards rushes from their station in the right-hand tower, kicking into attention in front of me. He holds three spread fingers against his forehead in salute.

"Captain Barnacle," he shouts over his shoulder, "the princess is home!"

"Good evening, Cid," I reply, hiding my annoyance like a good princess should and saluting back so he'll relax. Not that he does. He's too excited. I suppose it was too much to hope that we could slip into the palace unnoticed, get the separation, and then return to Seaview with no one but Daddy having to know. "How have you been?"

At nearly ninety, Cidaris is approaching retirement age—merfolk are extremely long-lived—but Daddy would never ask him to retire. He's more like family than royal guard.

"Wonderful, thank you, Princess," he replies, still at attention. "Your visit is an unexpected surprise."

For you and me both, Cid.

Barney emerges from the tower, straightening the collar on his uniform jacket as he hurries to Cid's side.

"I informed the palace," he announces.

But I don't think Cid hears a word Barney said, because he finally notices the cargo on my back. His eyes widen a little in realization, and then he smiles. An I-just-won-the-lottery smile.

"Oh, Princess," he says. He softens all over and rushes forward to give me a hug, grabbing Quince in his embrace too.

"I'm so very happy for you. Your father will be thrilled."

Sure he will. When I tell him I want a separation. If he didn't approve of any of the mermen who came to court me, many of them mer royalty, he's definitely going to be thrilled to send Quince packing.

"Oh my," Barney says. "Oh my, oh my, oh my." Then he rushes back into the tower, presumably to give the palace a bubble message update.

Great! Why does everything have to be a giant spectacle? In my time as an average, almost-invisible, nonroyal normal girl at Seaview, I've happily forgotten how every little detail of my life gets blown out of proportion down here. This isn't breaking news. It's a mistake. Bad luck. Nothing special. Quince is just a regular boy. A rude, obnoxious, tormenting regular boy. Who leans close and whispers in my ear, "What was that you wanted to tell me?" He pauses, his soft lips warm against my ear sending shivers all over, before adding, "*Princess?*"

I am *never* going to hear the end of this.

Margarite, the palace housekeeper, meets us at the door.

Instead of showing us to Daddy's office, where he spends practically every waking hour and occasional sleeping ones, she leads us to the ballroom. She is glowing like a flashlight fish. For the palace gossip queen, Quince and I must be like the best present ever. The entire kingdom will know within minutes. Well, at least I won't be here to deal with the cleanup. We'll talk to Daddy—correction, *I'll* talk to Daddy. I don't trust Quince to open his mouth without winding up with a trident shoved up his— Wait, why did I think that was a bad idea?

Anyway, after Daddy hears the circumstances, he'll grant the separation in a heartbeat, and biker boy and I will be escorted back to the mainland before sunrise. If the sea gods are smiling on me, Quince will have a black eye to show for his efforts.

"Lily!"

I whip around to see Daddy swimming down from the second floor.

I didn't realize how very much I've missed him until right now. For a second, I drink in the sight of him. He looks regal, as usual, with his graying hair trimmed shorter than the last time I was home. Tonight he's wearing his Thalassinian navy dress uniform—a pale blue jacket decorated with pearl buttons and a variety of ribbons and shells of commendation—and looks one hundred percent the high and mighty king. Except for the smile that pops onto his face when he sees me.

"Daddy!" I squeal, and kick over to meet him at the base of the ramp. His arms wrap around me, cocooning me in his strong, protective shell. I nuzzle my cheek against his neck, and he rubs his over the top of my head. I always feel safe in Daddy's arms. Nothing can hurt me.

"I have missed you," he murmurs against my hair. "You

97

should not stay away so long."

"I missed you too, Daddy," I reply, pulling back so I can look at his handsome face. The lines of maturity around his eyes look deeper than last time. "I just got so busy with schoolwork and the news team that I barely had time to sleep."

"But you're here now." He releases me and grins. He looks years younger.

Back by the ballroom doors, Quince clears his throat. Loudly. I close my eyes and clench my teeth. I knew he couldn't keep his mouth shut.

"Daddy, this is—"

My dad jets away with a powerful kick before I can finish. I hurry after him, to stop him from killing Quince before I get a chance to explain. In an instant he's in front of Quince, reaching for him. Oh, no, he's going to choke the life out of him. *Before* we break the bond.

"Daddy, no," I shout, moving to intervene. "He's not—"

My jaw drops.

Daddy's not strangling Quince. He's *hugging* him!

I drift the rest of the way, staring in complete shock as my dad embraces the bane of my existence, who catches my eye over Daddy's shoulder and winks. Well, if Daddy's not going to strangle him, I will.

"What's your name, boy?" Daddy demands, releasing Quince and pulling on his imposing king-of-the-ocean persona.

"Fletcher, sir," he replies. "Quince Fletcher."

Leave it to the blowfish to act all polite and respectful.

"Well, Quince Fletcher." Daddy throws one arm around Quince's shoulders and the other around mine, squeezing us together. "Welcome to the family."

10

"**I** can't believe he said that," I mutter for the quadrillionth time. "I can't believe he *said* that. I can't *believe* he—"

"I get it," Peri interrupts. "You're in disbelief. Can we just stipulate the point and move on?"

Guess I know what Peri's legal vocabulary word of the week is.

"But Peri," I whine, "Daddy . . . *likes* him."

Across the crowded ballroom I see Daddy introducing Quince to the members of the royal council, the ten most powerful merfolk in Thalassinia other than the king. They're all smiling and laughing and nodding like they've never been happier.

I've never been more miserable.

Nothing about the last twenty-four hours has gone according to plan. First, the blowfish lures me into the library—as if I buy the whole Brody-was-too-busy-dancing thing. Then he kisses me. *Then* he can't even swim! Now he's convinced my dad and the entire Thalassinian royal court—the *entire* court!—that he's my perfect mermate.

"Why didn't you tell your dad it was an accident?" Peri asks.

"I tried," I say, reliving those confusing moments in the hall. "But before I could say anything, he threw open the ballroom doors and—" I cover my face with my hands. "Well, you heard the announcement."

"Who didn't?"

"My daughter has bonded!" he shouted to the entire court assembled for my cousin Dosinia's sixteenth-birthday ball. I'd completely forgotten about the party. Could the timing be any worse? (Oh, wait, this is *my* life we're talking about, so clearly not.) The crowd's cheer must have registered on tsunami warning systems on both sides of the Atlantic. Then, before I could blink, we were being passed around the room, getting hugs and congratulations from everyone.

When Uncle Portunus grabbed Quince in a giant bear hug, I made my escape to the buffet table. Peri pulled me out from behind the tower of candy-coated sand strawberries and beach plums. To my surprise, no one at the party came after me. They all seemed focused on meeting Quince.

"After the party," I say. "I'll explain everything as soon as Dosinia's party is over."

"How considerate of you," a cold voice says from behind

me. "You should win the cousin-of-the-year award."

I twist around to find Dosinia floating under a swag of seaweed streamers, arms crossed over her well-displayed— maybe sponge-enhanced—chest, and glaring at me. She may be twenty-two months younger than me, but she's always acted way superior. And way hateful. Like my primary purpose in life is to make her miserable, when it's more like the other way around.

"Too bad you didn't wait to show up *after* my party," she snaps.

"I'm sorry, Doe," I say, even though I know she won't accept an apology. "I didn't mean to crash your party. I totally forgot it was even happening tonight."

I know I've said the wrong thing when her eyes—piercing blue surrounded by a thick ring of squid-ink liner—narrow menacingly.

"I didn't mean tha—"

"Nice to know my major milestones rank so highly on your social calendar," she snaps. "I'll be sure to return the favor on your next birthday."

With a flick of her tail fin, she jets over me and Peri, sending a bowlful of cocktail shrimp swirling around us. This just isn't my day. Or my week. Or maybe my life.

No, sadly, this *is* my life.

"Don't sweat Dosinia," Peri says, trying to soothe me like a best friend does. "She's been a sea witch all week. My mom nearly told her to go have someone else make her coming-out gown. And you know how much Mom will take before she blows her top."

Peri's mom is practically a saint, but Doe could try the patience of Old Man River himself.

"Doe means well," I say, mainly trying to reassure myself. As my only girl cousin, she should be like a sister. "Tonight is a big night for her. And I totally ruined it."

I do feel sorry for her. This was supposed to be her huge debut, her official introduction to the royal court and an invitation for eligible mermen to begin courting her— not that Doe hasn't been dating for years, but now it's official. Suitors will be lining up to woo her, guaranteed. First, because she's the king's niece. Considering how Daddy scared away all *my* prospective suitors, that's as close to the throne as most eligible young mermen will get. And second, she's gorgeous. With her long, caramel blond hair, hot pink and purple fins, full glossy lips, and eyes that could hypnotize a boy in under twenty seconds, she'll have her pick of the kingdom.

Tonight should have been about her, not the blowfish biker boy with broad shoulders and an enchanting smile and—

"Then I dragged her into the stall and pulled her onto my lap," Quince says, loud enough for me to hear halfway across the ballroom.

The entire assembly, listening with rapt attention, bursts out laughing. Even Daddy.

"I'm going to kill him," I tell Peri as I kick off toward the group.

As I swim up, he's saying, "So there she is, tears streaming down her face, but still ready to—"

"There you are!" I shout over what he's about to say. I swim down to his side and wrap an arm around his waist, squeezing tight and digging my fingernails into the flesh of his rib cage. "Why don't we let the council members go congratulate Dosinia on her debut? You can tell your stories later."

I give him a look that clearly states that by "later," I mean "never." Not that he takes any of my hints. He gets that infuriating self-assured smile on his face, slides one strong arm around my shoulders, and squeezes back. His eyes hold mine captive as he says, "Whatever you say . . . *Princess*."

I smile through gritted teeth, waiting for his audience to drift away so I can tell him what I'm really thinking. Although I bet he can guess.

When we're somewhat alone, I say, "Do *not* embarrass me in front of my people. I'm a member of the royal family, and I will not have my dirty gossip spread throughout the seven seas."

His eyes soften, and all that obnoxious cockiness melts away. "I wasn't trying to—"

"Well, you were," I insist. "And while you may never have to see these people again, I have to live the rest of my life here, and I don't want them snickering about me behind my back or doubting my judgment."

"I'm sorry," he says, sounding sincere. "It won't happen again."

"Good."

I'm not sure how to deal with an apologetic Quince. Especially when something in my gut tells me his remorse is real. This knowledge stuns me for a second—even knowing the bond is creating this connection, it feels so . . . natural.

"The rest of your life, huh?" he asks, popping my focus.

"What?"

"You're moving back here permanently," he says, his emotions now carefully guarded. "When? After graduation?"

"Probably—"

"There's the happy couple!" Daddy swims over, his two closest advisers in his wake.

I still can't get over how happy he looks. I don't get it. Every merboy I even spared a second glance got the third degree and threats of deportation to the Mariana Trench— the merworld equivalent of Siberian salt mines. But Quince shows up, this idiotic, obnoxious human, and Daddy's practically throwing a parade.

Why is this time different?

Now it's going to break his heart when he learns this is all a huge mistake. Better to clear things up now, before he gets too attached.

"Daddy, I need to tell you—"

"There is some paperwork to fill out," he interrupts.

"Some forms and waivers that you and Quince"—he throws Quince a proud smile—"must fill out before the joining ceremony."

"But Daddy—"

"No point in putting it off," he continues. "My advisers have prepared the documents."

"Daddy—"

"Won't take but a few minutes."

"Da—"

"We can go to my office right now and—"

"It was a mistake!" I shout, way louder than I intended, but he just wasn't listening. What else was I supposed to do?

Besides, it works. Daddy stops talking. He stops smiling, too. In fact, he's kind of frowning—no, make that scowling.

That's when I realize the entire ball has fallen silent around us. Not even the current stirs as I feel all attention on me. I squeeze my eyes shut. The entire assembly just heard my outburst . . . and now they're eagerly awaiting the next move.

"My office," Daddy roars. "Now!"

He jets off, expecting us to follow. I glare at Quince, because even if he didn't know what he was getting into, this is all his fault. Graysby and Grouper grab Quince, one at each arm, and carry him to the door and out into the hall. Leaving me completely alone in a room full of people staring at me. As I turn to follow, I catch Peri's gaze across the room. She gives me a sympathetic smile, knowing I'm in for some kind of tirade. Then, without looking at any of the other dozens of pairs of eyes watching me, I flick my way to the door and head for Daddy's tower office.

I was fully prepared to deal with a furious father when I got home. Just not one who was furious because I *wasn't* bonding to a human. Maybe it's the full moon that's making everything and everyone go all swirly.

I can't think of anything that could conceivably make this situation worse.

Daddy is pacing up a whirlpool when I swim into his office. Quince is sitting on one of the two chairs facing Daddy's massive desk. Although merfolk don't really need chairs— who needs to sit when you can float?—they are a ceremonial holdover from Poseidon's court.

As I swim around to take the other chair, Quince gives me an apologetic smile. My anger at him deflates a little. (It's always harder to hold on to my irritation underwater.) He's gotten swept up in this just as much as anyone else, but I can sense that he feels bad for getting me in trouble.

Great, the bond is totally broadcasting his emotions. Next thing you know, I'll be reading his thoughts, too. We need to get this thing severed before the line between what's real and what's the bond turns into total murk.

107

"Daddy," I begin. "I—"

"Silence!"

I sink into the chair next to Quince. Being the daughter of the king, I learned a long time ago to keep my mouth shut when he's on a rampage.

Daddy takes a few deep breaths, and that seems to calm him. Then, with a gentler expression on his face, he settles into the ornate chair behind his desk. His hands grip the curved arms so tightly that his knuckles turn white, but his face is completely calm.

He's trying to act like Daddy, but I can tell His Royal Highness King Whelk is lurking just beneath the surface.

"Please explain how this"—he gestures at me and Quince—"is a 'mistake.'"

"Well, Daddy, there's this boy—"

"No," he interrupts. Pointing at Quince, he says, "I'd like him to tell me what happened."

Quince leans forward in his seat and nods, like he understands what's going on here. Good, that makes one of us. Must be a guy thing.

"It was my fault, sir," he says, sounding all respectful. "Your daughter was expecting to meet another young man, but when he was unable to make the appointment, I arrived instead."

I gape at Quince. Who is this guy sitting in my father's office? And what has he done with the obnoxious biker boy I brought to Thalassinia? This guy is all big words and

108

respect and reverence. Nothing like the Quince I know on land.

Maybe water's mellowing him, too.

"And the kiss?" Daddy growls.

I wince. Is there any greater torture than sitting there listening as your first kiss—I still can't believe that, for the rest of my life, my first kiss will always have been Quince Fletcher—tells your dad all about the experience? Humans should feel grateful they can keep theirs a secret.

"My apologies, sir," Quince says. "I don't feel comfortable discussing the details of a very private moment. But I can assure you that I am entirely to blame for the situation. Lily could not have guessed that I would kiss her."

My breath rushes out in a relieved whirl. I'll have to thank Quince for that small favor. Although, if I'm being honest, I kind of wonder what Quince thought of the kiss. My fins curled—because I *thought* he was Brody—but what about him? Was it just another kiss?

Daddy doesn't speak, just nods. Elbows resting on the arms of his chair, he steeples his fingers together beneath his chin. His stormy gray eyes have a faraway look, and I can tell he's trying to figure out what to do. Well, I can tell him what to do. Perform the separation ritual so Quince and I can go home and get back to our regular lives.

Not that I say anything.

"All right, I'll grant the separation," Daddy finally says. Then, before I can squeal for joy—not that I expected him to do anything else—he adds, "Tomorrow night."

I gawk. "What?"

"Can you remain overnight without complications?" he asks Quince, ignoring my outburst.

Quince nods. "Yes, sir."

"You may go," Daddy says, waving Quince away. "I would like to speak with my daughter privately."

Quince pushes out of the chair and tries to paddle across the room to the door. But, as he said earlier, he can't swim. So he just floats slowly across the room, propelled by his shove against the chair. It's painful to watch. When I can't take it anymore, I kick out of my chair and swim to his side.

"You have to cup the water," I explain. "Like this."

I demonstrate a simple pull stroke. He copies me, but the water just slips between his fingers.

"Keep your fingers together." I take his hand, molding it watertight so he can actually get some propelling motion going. "Now try."

This time when he pulls, he moves—in a circle, because he just pulled one hand, but it's still progress. He tries again with both hands, sending himself floating toward the door. He looks back over his shoulder as he strokes away, flashing me an inscrutable grin. "Thanks, princess."

I'm not sure how I can tell, but I don't think he was mocking my title. I watch until he makes it to and through the door, where Graysby and Grouper try to carry him again. The last thing I see before the door shuts is Quince shrugging them off, saying, "I got this."

I don't realize until I turn back to Daddy that I'm smiling. My face immediately goes blank.

"Daddy, you can't really expect him to—"

"This isn't about your young man," he says, swimming out from behind his desk and pulling me into an embrace. "As soon as I perform the separation, you will go rushing back to the surface. I'd like us to spend some time together before you go."

Leave it to Daddy to say the one mushy thing that makes me okay with his decision. His request reminds me just how long I've been gone, how much I've missed the sea. If only it had been Brody in the library, then we could stay permanently.

I wonder briefly what Daddy's reaction will be when I finally bring Brody home. Will he be just as surprisingly enthusiastic as he has been about Quince?

"Tell me something." I lean back, curiosity getting the better of me.

"Anything," he says automatically.

"Why do you like him?" I have great faith in Daddy's judgment, so it's a total mystery why he's treating Quince like his long-lost son-in-law. A tiny niggle of doubt at the back of my mind wonders if maybe Daddy sees something in him that I haven't seen. "Why did you welcome him with open arms when you worked so hard to scare away every merboy in the sea?"

Daddy nudges aside a lock of blond hair that's drifted into my eyes. "Because I thought you'd chosen him," he says. "All those silly merboys pursued you, so I could never be certain of their intentions. But you brought this boy, a terraped who could have no real concept of your position in our society. He couldn't be just another title chaser."

"Oh," I say quietly. I don't know why a part of me is disappointed. It's not like I wanted him to tell me Quince was some kind of magically perfect mermate or anything. Besides, this is good news, because the situation will be the same with Brody. I should feel relieved.

No, I *do* feel relieved. This is great. The blowfish and I will stay the night, I'll get to hang out with Daddy for a while. Then I can go back to Seaview knowing that when I finally bring Brody home, he'll get a celebratory welcoming.

As I snuggle back in against Daddy's neck, I ask, "Will you take me to Bubbles and Baubles?"

He heaves a big sigh, but I know it's just pretend irritation. Daddy loves spoiling me whenever I'm home.

"Only if you promise to leave *some* stock in the store this time," he says. "You can't possibly take that much back to your aunt's."

"That's okay," I tease. "I'll just leave anything I can't carry in my room here."

Daddy clears his throat and pulls back. "Yes, we need to discuss your room."

My room? What's to discuss?

"With all the guests in town for Dosinia's ball, we've had to"—he pauses, like he's looking for the right words—"be creative in our accommodations."

"How creative, exactly?" I ask, not liking the sound of this.

"After some necessary rearrangements and last-minute guests, all but one of our guest rooms are full. Quince will obviously have to stay in the available room. Unfortunately," he says, "you will not have yours to yourself."

11

"*L*et me stay with you," I beg Peri. "We can have a sleep-over like when we were guppies."

"Can't," she says. "The whole extended family is in town for the ball. I'm already sharing my room with three of my cousins."

I roll over and bury my head in hot pink sea anemones—a special stingless variety cultivated by the royal seascape artist exclusively for the palace gardens. They don't have a scent, but their velvety-soft petals feel like satin against my cheek. I'm in desperate need of some serious Zen. Just when I thought my weekend couldn't get any worse.

"She'll kill me in my sleep," I complain.

"No, she won't."

"You don't know that, Peri," I insist. "She hates me. This is the opportunity she's been waiting for all her life."

"You're royalty," Peri says, as if that makes everything better. "Dosinia knows that killing you would be high treason. She might dye your hair purple, but she won't kill you."

Leave it to Peri to be all logical in a situation like this. Sharing my room—*my* room—with Dosinia is like moving in with a great white shark who has a taste for mermaid.

Dosinia and I should be close. Growing up, we should have teamed up against our boy cousins. Kitt and Nevis were (still are) total nightmares who put spider crabs in our beds and jellyfish in our sandwiches. Even though they were just as mean to Doe, she always liked them more than she liked me. Played with them instead of me. I've never understood why.

"Maybe I can just sleep out here in the gardens," I suggest. "We've done it before."

"Be serious, Lily." Peri picks a caulerpa frond and slides it behind my ear. "With the spring current as strong as it is right now, you'd be in Bermuda by morning."

"This is so unfair." I know I'm whining, but I don't care. "It's *my* room."

"Stop whining." Peri pulls my head out of the anemones. "You still haven't told me all the juicy details about your terraped cargo." She glances at the palace gate, where Cid and Barney are showing Quince how to drive a wakemaker (like a golf cart but water powered). "He's cute."

I jolt up. "He is *not* cute."

115

Peri gives me a look that says, You've got to be kid-ding me.

"All right." I scowl. At her and partly at him. "He's not hideous looking."

She lifts one elegantly curved brown eyebrow.

"He's . . ." I narrow my gaze in his direction just as the wakemaker takes off, leaving him flipping backward through the water. Rather than act upset or hurt, Quince spins out laughing. His big, bright smile gleams in the bioglow from across the gardens. When he catches me looking, he gives me two thumbs up, like that was the coolest thing ever. "He's got assets," I finally—and very, very reluctantly—concede. "He has a nice smile."

Not as nice as Brody's, of course, but no one's is.

"The boy's a certified hunk," Peri says, sizing up Quince like a slice of kelpberry pie. Then she turns to me, pinning me down with her gray-green gaze. "But last I knew, you were full-on hooked by Brody the swim wonder. How'd you wind up bonded to the neighbor boy?"

I give her the brief play-by-play—without the part about my fins curling or how nice and warm his lips felt or how he made me kiss him again before going underwater or how he didn't have to try that hard to *make* me. When I'm done, she doesn't say a word. Just plucks another frond, rolls onto her back, and lets it flutter in the current.

"Well?" I prod.

"Well what?" she replies.

"Don't you think that sucks rotten fish eggs?" Why isn't my best friend commiserating with me about how awful this situation is? Shouldn't she be outraged at his forward behavior and agreeing that we should have a pair of dolphins drop him in the Arctic? I kick up from the anemones and twist around so I'm floating in front of her. "I've told you the stories. Like about the time he spent a week following me to and from school on his motorcycle—never said a word, just rumbled along ten feet behind me the whole way. And that he slams my locker shut *every* time he walks by. And how he always manages to ruin every possible moment of progress I make with Brody. I mean, don't you think he's the worst slime to ever sink fin on the ocean floor? He's just so mean and rude and—"

"Floating right behind you," Peri says, not looking away from her anemone grooming.

I freeze. Maybe she is just messing with me. Or she's mistaken. Or—

"Talking about me, *Princess*?"

Of course. I close my eyes and gulp in a deep breath before spinning around. "Quince, I—"

"No harm, no foul," he says, waving off my apology. He's playing like it's no big, but I see something in his eyes— I sense something in him—that says it's bigger than he's admitting. I *feel* it. He doesn't relent, though. "That wake-maker is some piece of power." He gestures back toward the gate, where Cid and Barney are now trying to wrestle

117

the wakemaker back into the tower garage.

"Yeah," I agree, trying to make up for acting like a sea witch by being extra nice. "It takes a little getting used to. The trick is letting out the clutch real slow."

He flashes me another brilliant smile. "I'll remember that next time."

Peri makes a really loud yawning noise behind me. "Time for me to head home," she says. "Gotta get the little cousins tucked into bed."

"Do you have to go now?" I spin around, pleading with my eyes for her to stay. To not leave me alone with Quince.

"Yes." She gives me a meaningful look, one that says, I can't save you all the time. "Besides, between Doe's party and your"—she shrugs at Quince—"return, I'm wiped out. I'll be asleep before I float through the door."

Then, before I can argue or beg or threaten blackmail, she waves good night and swims away. I watch her disappear through the gates. It's not like I've never been alone with Quince before, but now it feels different. Now he knows the truth about me—the whole *royal* truth—and I'm beyond nervous about facing him.

Finally I turn around.

"I—"

"I'm wiped, too," he says before I have to make verbal sense of my thoughts, saving me from saying something stupid. "Your dad said you'd show me to the starfish room?"

"Sure," I say, my stomach sinking a little. I'm not sure why I feel bad that he's giving me an easy out for the night. I mean, I don't want to hang out with him. Right? "It's one floor down from my room in the southwest tower."

We swim in silence to the palace main entrance. It's slow going because he's trying to swim on his own, but he's getting better. He's figured out how to combine the simple breaststroke pull with a dolphin kick. Still way slower than my normal speed, but pretty impressive for a human who couldn't swim this morning.

I get the feeling he's really trying to make the best of this. Which only makes me feel worse for ripping on him to Peri.

"You know, I didn't mean what I said," I explain, filling the silence as we move through the main hall and toward my tower. "I don't really think you're mean and rude. Well, not mean, anyway. You can be a little rude, but that's no excuse for my—"

"Lily."

I'm not sure what stops my babbling apology—it could be his commanding tone or the fact that he's used my actual name for once. Either way, my mouth snaps shut.

"It's okay." He doesn't look at me as he speaks, which makes me feel like even more of a sea slug. "Really. I know you didn't ask for this situation any more than I did. I won't hold your emotions against you."

"I——" I can't believe what he just said. It was just so . . . nice. "Thank you. I really am sorry, though. I just want to get through tomorrow, get the separation, and then get back to our regular lives."

"Back to Brody."

"Yes," I say, ignoring the chill in his voice, the sudden tension in his body. "Back to Brody. Back to Seaview. Back to everything that was normal before last night's dance. It's not about you," I explain. Not *entirely* about him, anyway. "It's about me. That's all."

Quince stops swimming and looks directly into my eyes. "I get it, princess. Really I do." One side of his mouth lifts in a mocking smile. "I want to get back to normal too."

There are some serious undertones in his last statement; I'm just not sure what they are.

Several seconds tick by as we look at each other, like we're both trying to figure out what's really going on. For the first time, I actually try to tap into the bond, to reach out and read what he's feeling. I focus in on Quince and open my mind to him.

I'm struck by a sudden sense of longing that is much stronger than anything I'm feeling. Is that how badly he wants to get home?

I feel even worse for being so angry at him. All he did was kiss the wrong girl, and in an instant his life on land was yanked away. The least I can do is help him have a good time while he's here.

120

"So where's this starfish room?" he asks, bursting our intensity bubble.

Without a word, I turn and swim for my tower, knowing Quince will follow.

"This is it," I say. A quick twist of the handle, and I push inside what has always been one of my favorite rooms in the palace. I have kind of a thing for stars of any kind—probably because we can't see the real stars from the ocean floor. You have to swim to the surface to see them twinkling above. Besides having the predictable starfish-shaped accessories, the starfish room has a bioluminescent-painted ceiling of stars. As I float into the room, I twist onto my back and gaze up at the starry surface. It makes me a little homesick for land.

But, now I know, not nearly as homesick as Quince.

"This is a bedroom?" Quince asks, floating in after me. "Where's the bed?"

"There." I point at the shell-shaped piece in the center of the room.

"O-kay. . . ." He swims over and eyes the bed skeptically. Not your typical box-spring four-poster, sure, but if I could get used to sleeping on a flat mattress, he can spend one night in a curved shell. Then, as he awkwardly turns to inspect the room, his gaze lands on the sculpture in the corner. "Whoa."

"It's beautiful, isn't it?" I ask. We both swim over to the three-dimensional, twisting column made of every variety of blue shell found in the sea. My favorites are the sand dollars, dotting the deep blue swirl with spots of brighter, almost sky-colored blue.

Quince runs a hand hesitantly over the curves, as if he might accidentally send all the shells scattering into the current. Then I hold my breath as his fingertips linger over one of the sand dollars.

"Such a bright blue," he says. "I've never seen them this color."

I try to ignore the fact that he's fixating on my favorite part of the sculpture. Instead, I focus on being educational. "Sand dollars are naturally very colorful," I explain. "But when they die, they gradually pale to the white shade we see on land."

"Then are these"—he touches one gently—"alive?"

"No." The thought of a living sculpture makes me smile. It's a pretty cool idea, but keeping the shelled creatures alive and in place would be a major effort. "The artist treated recently deceased sand dollars to maintain the color. It's a flash-freeze technique that can preserve anything from sand dollars to starfish to yards of rainbow-colored seaweed."

"That's amazing," he says, turning his awe-filled gaze on me. "*You* are amazing."

No, I think, I'm just an average mermaid. But when he looks at me like that, I almost *feel* amazing.

"Sleep as late as you like," I blurt, uncomfortable with the sudden comfortableness of the situation. The longer he sleeps, the less time I have to spend trying to figure out what to say to him. The less the chance I'll say something mean or stupid. "I'll find you before the ceremony tomorrow night. Until then, just lay low and—"

"Hold on," he interrupts. "You think I'm just going to stay curled up in your guest room all day? No way. If I only get a once-in-a-lifetime chance to explore a mermaid kingdom, I'm not wasting the opportunity. I want to see . . . everything."

"Be serious, Quince." I try to reason with him. "You can't just swim around Thalassinia, looking in houses and—"

"I know." Quince swims close, so close that I can feel his body heat in the water. "You can show me around."

"Uh-uh." I shake my head. The last thing I want to do is spend more time in his company. Especially with the bond messing with our emotions—or at least mine. I'm already softening toward him, even though I *know* it's just the bond.

"Come on, princess," he murmurs, floating closer still. "I've been pretty good about this whole mermaid thing. I think I've earned a personal tour."

My shoulders slump. He has me there. He *is* taking this really well. No tantrums or freak-outs or even disbelief. And if I were in his shoes—or rather, his biker boots—I'd want to take a look around, too.

"Fine." I relent. "I'll give you the royal tour."

He grins, and I have to consciously stop myself from smiling back. No good can come from forming a stronger connection with Quince.

"I'll meet you in the breakfast room," I suggest. "We can leave from there."

I turn away before his smile infects me. I'm almost through the door when he says, "Good night, Princess."

Without turning around, I say, "Night, Quince."

As I swim up to my room, I wonder how it happened that Quince and I are actually being civil to each other. Clearly, the bond can make miracles happen.

Dosinia is floating outside my room—*our* room, I remember with a groan—when I get upstairs. Like she's been waiting for me.

"Getting a good-night kiss from your bond boy?" She crosses her arms over her chest and kicks one hip to the side. "He's decent looking, I suppose. If you go for terrapeds."

"Drop it, Doe," I say, pushing past her and into the room. "I'm not up for this right now."

"Oooh, trouble in paradise?" She hurries in after me, hovering as I swim to my dresser and pull open the bottom drawer, looking for a sleep shirt.

The drawer is full of sequin- and pearl- and glitter-covered tops. Definitely not my style.

"Where are my clothes?" I demand. Jerking open the other three drawers, I find them all equally full of Dosinia's frilly and borderline-trampy wardrobe. The girl does not get the concept of understatement.

"Sorry," she singsongs, swimming over to the bed and

floating down onto the spongy mattress. "I had to put my clothes *somewhere*."

Scowling, I repeat, "Where?"

She gestures at the big steamer trunk under my window. It was a present from Daddy for my twelfth birthday. He'd salvaged the trunk from an old shipwreck and had it restored and waterproofed so it wouldn't fall apart. I flip open the shiny gold latches and pull up the lid, only to find the entire contents of my dresser tossed into the trunk in a giant messy pile. I don't have the energy for a fight, so I just grab a top and head for the bathroom.

Doe follows me.

"He's not your usual type," she says from the open doorway. "You usually go for the mossy-mouthed, untouchably popular guys. This one seems like he knows where to find trouble without much looking."

She sounds . . . intrigued. That's the last thing I need.

"Let it go, Doe," I beg. I duck behind the bathing curtain and change out of my tank top. "He's only here for a day. Not worth setting your hooks into."

"If you say so."

When I emerge, she's not in sight. A quick peek into the room, and I see her slam my trunk shut.

She acts like such a guppy.

"Why did you have to come back tonight?"

I can't see her eyes because her back is to me, but I can tell from the tone of her voice that she's on the verge of tears.

When a mermaid cries underwater, it's not like on land. Her tears just dissolve into the water around her, mixing their salty drops into the salty sea. The only indication that she's crying is her eyes. No matter what color her irises are usually, when she cries they turn into a sparkling shade that matches her scales. I know from experience that mine turn gold. And Dosinia's turn bright pink. Like the anemone field in the garden below.

"I didn't have a choice," I explain, swimming around behind her. "I had to get him here as quickly as possible so I could get the separation and move on with my life. It's just . . . bad luck that it happened to be tonight." I place one hand on her shoulder, next to her fuchsia-colored mer mark. "I didn't mean to ruin your party."

She laughs and shrugs off my hand. "Ruin?" she asks like it's a ridiculous notion. "Are you kidding? It was the social event of the year."

She turns and looks me in the eye for a split second before jetting over to the bed and settling in on what has always been *my* side. But rather than argue—about the bed or the party—I just quietly take the other side and sink in. Besides, how do you argue with a girl whose eyes are sparkling brighter than the moon?

12

Quince eyes the breakfast buffet in the main dining hall as if it might get up and swim away. I don't know what his problem is. The spread looks amazing. There are mounds of scrambled eel eggs, toasted sea fans, strips of pickled kelp, and a variety of local fruit mixed with some land fruit—the kingdom has a trading agreement with some human merchants who prize the giant conch and other shells we can provide. And, if you love sushi—I dare you to name a mermaid who doesn't love sushi—we have just about every variety of nigiri, maki, and inari you could dream of.

Grabbing a plate, I start piling on Thalassinian delicacies.

"Care to introduce me to the menu, princess?"

I scowl at Quince, ready to deflect whatever insult he's getting ready to hurl, but he looks genuinely concerned about the buffet.

"You don't eat sushi, do you?" I guess.

"Not if I can avoid it."

Rolling my eyes, I point out the eel eggs and sea-fan toast. "Take some of those." I scoop up a spoonful of fruit and dump it on his plate. "This should get you through the day without having to resort to raw fish."

He gives me a relieved look and then piles on a plateful of my recommendations. I don't have the heart to tell him what they actually are. He'd probably put them back.

Once we're at the table and he's figured out how to use seasticks, the mer equivalent of chopsticks, he asks, "What's on the schedule?"

I shrug, dipping my spicy tuna maki in thick ginger sauce before placing the delight in my mouth. My eyes close automatically, focusing on the sensation of spicy and tangy on my tongue. The mainland has its fair share of sushi restaurants, and some of them are pretty passable. But nothing compares to the royal sushi master's concoctions. I feel my body hum with epicurean pleasure.

"That good, huh?"

My eyes flash open. In my bliss I've completely forgotten about Quince—about everything except pure sushi joy.

I chew and swallow quickly. Knowing my cheeks must be bright red, I keep my head down and catch another piece in my seasticks.

"Yes," I say simply.

I sense Quince shift next to me. "Then I have to try one."

Surprised, I look up at him. He looks serious.

"Hey, anything that gives a girl that kind of pleasure," he says with a wink, "has to be worth a try."

Now my cheeks are practically on fire. He watches me with a kind of unsettling intensity as I take the ginger-dipped piece I'd been about to eat and hold it out for him. For Quince.

Never taking his eyes off me, he leans forward and opens his mouth. The spicy tuna disappears between his full lips and white teeth. My eyes dart up, anxious to read his reaction. An array of emotion plays across his eyes. Uncertainty. Contemplation. Intrigue. Finally, in one fluid motion, he swallows, then gives me a slightly forced smile.

"Not the"—his smile wavers—"worst thing I've ever eaten."

"Oh," I say, not sure why I feel relieved. "Good."

"But I think I'll stick with the eggs and toast."

We finish the meal in silence. I watch Quince nervously out of the corner of my eye, waiting for him to realize that the "ketchup" he's putting on his eggs is actually sea-cucumber jelly, but he eats up ocean fare like it's his favorite burger and fries back home. Dosinia watches us carefully from across the table, trying to act completely uninterested, while everyone else in the royal household—from Daddy on down to Cid and Barry—watches me and Quince with undisguised fascination. I feel like a goldfish in a bowl, and I was fully prepared to face that reaction once I finally bonded. Only I'm stuck in my bowl with the wrong human.

Unable to force another bite of eel and salmon roe into my mouth when dozens of eyes in the room are watching my every move, I kick away from the table.

"Are you ready to go?" I demand, not waiting for Quince to respond before pulling him up and away from the last bites of sargassum grapes left on his plate. On land he may outmuscle me, like, three to one, but underwater I have the definite advantage of a massive strong tailfin and years of learning how to use it effectively.

I have him out of the dining hall before he protests. "In a hurry, princess?"

"Sorry." I don't mean it, but since I'm forcibly dragging him away from breakfast, I probably should. "I just couldn't sit there while everyone watched every tiny thing we did. I don't do well in the spotlight."

"Aren't you used to it?" he asks. "I mean, you're their princess. Haven't they always watched you like that?"

We pass into the front hall, and I finally release Quince to swim on his own. "Not like this," I explain. "They're all super eager because of the bonding."

Unconsciously I run my fingers through my hair. And, since it's not air frizzed, they actually rake through easily.

"Why does that make a difference?" he asks. "I mean, it's not like it was your first kiss."

My entire body from the waist up freezes. I'm still kicking, still moving toward the door, but I am otherwise motionless.

"Well, hell."

That freezes me altogether. I squeeze my eyes shut, as if that will make this whole situation disappear. As if I can pretend for a minute that I just came home for a nice visit, without a bonded Quince in tow. As if I can shut out the feelings of shock and (annoying) pride that are pouring out of him.

"I had no idea, Lily. If I had known, I would have—"

"Forget it," I snap, kicking back into motion. I can't take much more of this nice Quince. Rude, obnoxious Quince I can handle, but this is beyond my experience. "It's over. Done. We can't change what happened." Then, under my breath, I mutter, "No matter how much we want to."

Quince is silent for a minute, hopefully shocked by my outburst, but with my luck he's just building up steam. As we reach the front entrance, he wraps a warm hand around my arm and tugs me to a stop.

"Why did the bond make them watch you more intently?" he asks.

Maybe it's because there's no trace of mockery in his question, or because dealing with this kinder, gentler Quince is throwing me off my game, or because the bond is not only amplifying every emotion between us but also every physical sensation and the feeling of his hand on my arm is really,

131

really nice— Wait, where was I? Oh right. His question. For whatever reason, I give him a fully honest answer.

"Because in this world, a bond is the equivalent of marriage." I'm impressed that he doesn't betray a single emotion—in either his face or through our magical connection. "And because I'm a princess and the heir to the throne. One day I will be queen. They think I've chosen you as our future king, and they're trying to decide if I'm crazy or in love or just full-out stupid."

A little muscle along his jawline twitches, and there's a protective intensity in his eyes that pulls me in. I want to swim into those Caribbean-colored pools and never swim back out. That scares me.

Which is why I shrug out of his grip and turn away.

As I pull open the door, I hear him say, "And you wanted Brody to be the one at your side."

Now why does my body shiver all over when I realize Quince sounds jealous? It could be fear . . . or thrill (which scares me even more).

Thankfully I'm saved from responding.

"Princess Waterlily!" Cid hurries through the hall toward us. "Wait! Your father asks that you join him in court today," he gets out in gasping breaths.

Carpola, I forgot about Daddy wanting to hang out. "Oh, well, I was just going to show Quince around," I say. "He wanted to—"

132

"Don't sweat it," Quince says. "I'll amuse myself. Hang with your dad."

Although that might have sounded like a laid-back, cool kind of response, there is nothing laid-back about the steady tension swirling around him. I think it has nothing to do with me staying with Daddy and everything to do with that last statement about Brody. His masked jealousy pulls an echoing sympathy from me.

"His highness arranged for an alternative, Master Quince," Cid says. "The princess's cousin has volunteered to give you a tour."

On cue, Doe appears in the hall and swims over to Quince, linking her arm around his and looking me right in the eye as she says, "It would be my pleasure."

"Sounds great," Quince says, turning his attention to Dosinia with a charming smile. Son of a swordfish, what am I doing? Feeling sympathy for Quince's jealousy as if I think it's *real*? It's the bond. The last thing Quince Fletcher will ever be is jealous over me.

As they disappear out the front door, I ignore the sour feeling in my gut. After tonight, Quince will once again be nothing more than a pain in my tail fin. Dosinia can have him.

The Thalassinian throne room is a sight to behold. It is a cavernous dome-shaped room with amber-tinted torches (actually bioluminescent algae within amber glass balls) that cast a warm glow everywhere. The ceiling is covered with intricate coral carvings of sea monsters, ancient gods, and mer people, accented with finely applied gold leaf and coal shading. Under the torch glow, the gold sparkles and the shadows darken, making the carvings seem even deeper.

The floor beneath is a beautiful mosaic of pearly tiles that portray the founding of Thalassinia. At the center, Poseidon hands his trident to Capheira so she can tattoo her descendants with the mark of the mer, giving them the ability to transfigure into human form. She, in turn, spreads her hands to her people, who appear around her in various stages of transfiguration—some in pure terraped form, others fully mer, and still others as terraped with scale-covered finkinis in place. One of the mermen, my great-great-many-times-over-grandfather, is shown with one hand reaching back to his people, the other pressed to the seafloor. That spot he's touching is the exact spot on which the palace is built. The exact center of the throne room.

It always gives me a little thrill to feel that connection to the ancient past and our mythological origins.

"I've missed you, daughter," Daddy says as he takes his place on the throne. He motions me forward to take the smaller chair to his right. "You have stayed away too long."

"I'm sorry, Daddy." I swim up to him but don't take the offered seat. Instead, I float at his feet, like I did when I was a little mergirl. "Life on land can get really busy. It's like time is on super speed compared to Thalassinia's mellow-slow pace."

He thrums his fingers on the gilded arm of his throne. "I remember well the perpetual urgency of the terraped world. Perhaps it is because their lives are shorter than ours. They feel the need to pack much more into their time."

"Maybe." I muse, but I don't necessarily agree. Humans could live at a slower pace if they chose. With our extended life span, they would probably just move at their rapid pace for longer. It's a symptom of the world they've built.

"What do you have on your schedule today?" I ask. Although it's Sunday on the mainland, in Thalassinia it's the equivalent of a Monday. Our calendar is based on the lunar cycle, and Friday night's full moon—and the two days on either side—would have been our weekend. Daddy's Mondays are usually pretty busy.

"I have to hear a dispute about lobster grazing rights this morning," he explains. "But otherwise my calendar is clear. Perhaps we can go shopping in the afternoon."

"Oh. Should I go amuse myself and then come back after the hearing?" I ask. I'm not that thrilled at the idea of listening to two lobster farmers squabble about who gets to graze their herd on Horseshoe Crab Hill.

"No." Daddy's serious tone makes me look up. "I'd like you to participate. One day you will preside over these proceedings. You need the experience."

Panic washes through me. I'm not ready for this. I mean,

I've known my entire life that it is my destiny to take the throne, to rule over Thalassinia as generations of my family have done before. But I'm not ready *today*.

"Please." Daddy motions me to the chair on his right. "Take the queen's throne."

My heart stalls and the panic ebbs away, replaced by total emptiness.

"I—" I stare at Daddy and then the smaller version of his throne. The one made for the monarch's mate. The one made for my mom.

I can't sit there.

Not again.

One day, when I was about eight, Daddy let me play in the throne room while he met with his council in the palace conference hall. After exploring every inch of the carved ceiling and the mosaic floor, I gathered my Oceanista dolls—the mergirl equivalent of Barbie—and settled into the queen's throne to play fashion show. When Daddy returned and found me there, he got a sad look on his face, and his eyes sparkled royal blue to match his fins. I still hadn't forgotten that look in his eyes when I found out, years later, that it should have been my mother's throne.

I've never touched it since.

He watches me expectantly, waiting for me to take the seat by his side. I think we both know why I'm glued to my spot.

"I c-can't," I finally say.

Daddy's face softens. "She would have wanted you to."

He smiles like he's replaying a happy memory. "She would have been so proud to see you take the throne."

If we were on land, I would probably be angry. Furious that he gets to have memories of her that make him smile. A secret smile that I can never share. On land, my temper isn't soothed by the calming power of water. I'm much more . . . volatile. Underwater, my anger comes out as sorrow.

"What was she like?" I ask.

"She was . . ." His smile grows, and I see him drift back fully into memories. "Infectious. Always smiling, always laughing. You couldn't be around her and not be caught up in her joy."

I wish I had inherited that from her. Or maybe that's something you can't inherit—you have to learn it by watching. I never even got to see my mom smile.

"She was a remarkable woman."

"Would you do it all over again?" I ask. "Knowing how it would end, would you still choose her?"

Daddy takes my hands from his knees and pulls me up onto his lap. I feel like I'm that eight-year-old mergirl again, playing Oceanistas on the throne. He hugs his big arms around me and tucks me in close against his chest.

"Without hesitation," he says softly. "And I know your mother would say the same."

Even though I can't feel the tears, I know I'm crying. "Do you miss her?" I ask. "Do you still feel the bond, even though she's gone?"

"Yes, I miss her," he says, giving my shoulders a squeeze. "I gave her a piece of my heart and she took that with her." He holds me back, making me look into his eyes. "But not because of the bond. Your mother and I never bonded."

I jerk back. "What? Why not?"

"The situation was complicated," he explains. "At first, I didn't tell her the truth. As the king I had to be extremely cautious in my choice of mate, especially if she was a terraped. I wasn't about to force her into a life so foreign to hers. Then, by the time I knew she was my true mate and told her the truth, your grandmother had fallen terminally ill. Rachel was in the Peace Corps at the time, so the care of your grandmother fell to your mother."

The thought of Mom putting off her life to care for her dying mother brings fresh tears to my eyes. She was such a selfless person. I could never live up to that.

"In the meantime, you were born."

"Daddy!"

"Well, just because we didn't officially bond didn't mean we weren't committed and attracted to each other. We were young and in love," he explains. "No need to be scandalized."

Oh, but I *am* scandalized. That makes me accidentally kissing Quince more like a two on the scale of scandal.

"Anyway," he continues, "shortly after your birth, your grandmother passed." He stares out into the throne room, a blank look in his eyes. "We had everything planned. After the funeral, your mother would bring you to the beach. She and I would forge the bond, and then . . . well, we never got to that."

This part of the story I already know. On the way from Grandma's funeral, Mom got hit by a drunk driver. Some idiot who walked away without a scratch, while my mom went sailing through the windshield and into the path of an oncoming car. I was safely belted into a carrier in the backseat. Mom was the only one even injured in the five-car wreck.

"In some ways," Daddy says, coming back into the present, "I'm glad we never bonded. It is a small concession that my grief has never been compounded by an unfulfilled bond."

Across the room, one of the two massive gold doors swings open, and Mangrove, Daddy's royal secretary, peers in.

"Your highness," he says, reverently lowering his eyes— Daddy is so not the type to demand this kind of behavior, but Mangrove is kind of protocol obsessed. "The complainants are here."

"Give us a moment, Mangrove."

"Of course, your highness."

When Mangrove closes the door behind him, Daddy shakes his head. "That man is determined to act like a second-class citizen."

"Well, you can be very intimidating," I reply. "And you do carry a really big trident."

We both laugh a little, and it breaks the heaviness in the room. Then Daddy says, "Please. Take the throne, Lily."

Swimming off Daddy's lap, I float in front of Mom's throne. No one has sat on its spongy cushion in years. Somehow, as I remember everything Daddy said about Mom's selfless nature, it seems worse to see her throne abandoned than to feel like I'm usurping her rightful place. As I twist around and sink slowly into her seat, I think, This is for you, Mommy.

Daddy squeezes my hand before shouting, "Mangrove! Send them in!"

I square my shoulders and ready myself for my first session as ruler-in-training. If this is my future, I might as well start now.

13

*T*he thing you might not realize about lobster farmers—
especially if you're a human and you don't even
know there is such a thing—is that they smell like lobsters.
If you've only seen lobsters either cooked and ready to eat
or in one of those little tanks at a seafood restaurant, with
their claws rubber-banded, then you have no idea how bad
the stench of lobster can be. They make a cattle stockyard
seem like a rose garden.

So, after I spend most of the day listening to two quar-
reling farmers argue about fair grazing rights and whether
one had rebranded some of the other's herd, everything
in the throne room smells like lobster—including Daddy,
Mangrove, and me.

Thankfully, Margarite called in the housekeeping staff,
who unleashed a small school of surgeonfish—distant rela-
tives of those fish that eat scum out of aquariums—and they

141

managed to neutralize the smell in just a few minutes. I'm pretty sure my hair still has a little eau de lobster, but it's not like I'm going to let the surgeonfish suck on my head.

By the time the throne room is cleared, it's approaching evening. Approaching time for the separation—and Quince and Dosinia aren't back yet.

When night falls and the light filtering down from the distant surface is replaced with the bioluminescent glow of the palace lighting system, I start to worry. Not about going home in the dark; we'll have a royal escort of palace guards to keep us safe. But we have to be in school tomorrow, we still have a three-hour swim to get home—even though Quince's swimming ability has improved, he can't keep up with me—and we still have to get through the separation ceremony, which includes a mandatory couples counseling session. It's a formality, but still it takes time. And remember when I said that mer life is pretty mellow paced? Well that goes for ceremonies, too.

I start swimming circles around the throne. What if they don't come back? What if Dosinia is keeping Quince hostage as revenge for crashing her party? What if Quince got eaten by a shark? What if—

"Relax, daughter," Daddy says. "They will be back soon. There is nothing you can do to hurry their return."

"I know," I snap, "but I have a major trig test tomorrow. I haven't studied at all!"

142

"Your time with terrapeds has made you susceptible to their stress tendencies." He leans back in his throne, as casually as if he's watching a finball match. "Relax. If they have not returned in an hour, I will send the guard out."

"An hour?" That seems like forever from now. "We can't wait that long! We have to——"

The throne room doors swing open, and Mangrove announces, "Lady Dosinia and Master Quince have returned."

"Finally!"

Kicking off hard, I jet across the room, reaching the doors just as Quince and Dosinia swim in. They are laughing and holding hands.

"Then she screamed and spat half-chewed jellyfish all over the table!" Dosinia says. Both she and Quince burst into laughter—over an embarrassing story about me. Well, two can play at that game.

"Don't be telling tales, Doe," I say, swimming up to her and narrowing my gaze. "Or I might have to share about the time you thought the Loch Ness monster was hiding in your closet."

Quince, still laughing so hard he's probably crying—only I can't tell because human eyes don't sparkle—says, "Lighten up, princess. It was all in good fun."

I hold my glare on Dosinia. "Yeah. I'm sure."

As if Dosinia would ever do anything in good fun. She's still mad that I didn't invite her to my twelfth-birthday sleepover. Grudges are her specialty.

"Can't laugh at yourself, Lily?" she asks in a mocking tone. "How sad."

"Whatever." I turn away from her and grab Quince's hand. It's time to stop stalling. "We have a separation to attend."

As we swim away toward the throne, Quince shouts back over his shoulder, "Thanks for showing me around today, Doe."

My hand clenches tighter on his. How dare he use her nickname, like they're friends? Or . . . more.

"Anytime," Doe replies. "Next time you kiss a mermaid, maybe you can stay longer."

He laughs. She laughs. I jerk him faster toward the throne.

Brat. She knows that severing a human from the bond is a permanent thing. He'll be immune—to all mermaids, not just me. Not that I plan on ever accidentally kissing Quince again, but at least I know there's no way he'll end up in my court or anything.

"There won't be a next time," I mutter under my breath. Then, to Daddy, I say, "Let's get this over with."

He has his unreadable king-of-the-ocean face on, so I can't tell what he's thinking. I just hope he's thinking about getting this done as quickly as possible.

"Lily and Quince." He looks at each of us, then over our heads at Dosinia, still hovering by the door. She probably wants to gloat over the whole debacle of my accidental bonding.

When Daddy looks back down at me, I get a bad feeling

in my stomach. He has a little of that faraway look he had earlier when we were talking about Mom.

"I'm sorry," he says, quietly but firmly. "I cannot grant this separation."

Next to me, Quince frowns. Like he doesn't understand what just happened. That makes two of us.

"Daddy!" I shriek. I know I should be addressing him as the king right now, but he's acting like a dad, so I'll treat him as such. "What are you doing? You can't leave us bonded forever. You can't make him my king." Suddenly it makes sense. I float forward, and whisper, "Is this about my birthday? You can't tie me to him just so I don't lose my place in court. I can find a better mate."

In fact, I already have one lined up.

"It's not about that, Lily," he replies. His gaze flicks from Quince to Dosinia and back again. Otherwise, it's like we're alone in the room. This is just between Daddy and me.

"Our conversation about your mother," he says, "reminded me of the serious nature of bonding. A bond is a gift—a connection that has no equal in the seven seas and beyond. I can't just dissolve a bonding without cause. Especially when you obviously—"

"Without cause?!?" I start swimming up a whirlpool. "There is so much cause, I can't even begin to list it all. Did you know he throws paper wads at me? And peeps on me from his bathroom window? And last year he spent a week following me to and from school on his motorcycle—ooh, he rides a motorcycle, which is way more dangerous than a wakemaker. And he—"

"Enough!"

Daddy's royal shout echoes through the room. The witnesses to my humiliation freeze, afraid that the all-powerful king is making an appearance.

"My decision has been made," he states, in a tone that brooks no argument—although I'm ready to give him one. "You shall return to the sea in one week, and you will have an opportunity to prove that you should not be bonded for life. If I am satisfied that you are unsuitable, then I shall perform the separation at that time."

"But Daddy," I whine. "You can't—"

"I can," he says. "And I have." Then his face softens, and I know it's my dad speaking, not my king. "I want you to be one hundred percent certain about what you—"

"But I am certain," I insist. "Quince and I practically hate each other. He doesn't want to be bonded to me any more than I want to be stuck with him."

I glance at the boy in question. Why is he being so quiet about everything? Shouldn't he be speaking up in favor of the separation? Maybe he's too clouded by the bond.

"I know you believe you know your mind," Daddy says, "but I have doubts. I worry that you are letting other emotions interfere with the clarity of the bond. I will not perform the separation until I am satisfied that you truly

146

know what you want." He gives me a kingly look. "You will give the bond a week."

And that's that.

I know he means well. I mean, he's my dad. It's kind of his job to make decisions I hate because he thinks they're in my best interest. That doesn't make me like it.

But, as long as we're separated before the next lunar cycle begins, I suppose one week won't make that huge a difference in my life. Not in the long run. Not when I get to spend forever with the *real* boy of my dreams.

"One week," I agree. "For you." And, I add silently, for Mom.

Then, before anyone—me, probably—can get all weepy, I turn, grab Quince, and head for the doors.

As we swim past Dosinia, she waves. "See you next week, Quincy."

When I see him start to smile, I give a powerful kick and we're out of range before he can respond.

"Careful, princess," he says as we emerge into the gardens. "Someone might think you're jealous."

"You wish," I snap. The last person I would ever be jealous over is Quince Fletcher. I can't believe I have to spend a whole week bonded to this shark.

By the time Quince squeals his motorcycle into his driveway, my hair has dried into a frizzy frenzy. The section beneath the helmet is practically glued to my head, while the rest has blown out in all directions. I look like some crazy art experiment gone wrong. It'll take me an hour just to drag a brush through it all.

His bike rattles into silence.

I unwrap my arms from his torso, leap off the seat, and shove the helmet into his chest, ready to retreat into my house and bury my head under the pillows. But Quince isn't about to let me get away that easy. He wraps one strong hand around my wrist, shackling me to the spot.

"Not so fast, princess," he says, tugging me closer.

Rolling my eyes skyward, I notice the position of the moon. It's late. Too late for me to argue.

I give him a glare.

"I don't even rate a 'good night'?" Quince asks as I pull my wrist loose. "I think I've earned it."

I freeze.

How does he always know *just* what to say to totally set me off? I mean, it's like he has a special gift for pushing my buttons. Too bad it's not a marketable skill.

I'm sure it doesn't help that my temper's resurfaced because we're back on land or that I've had a few hours of silent swimming to build up my anger about the whole situation. Even though I know none of this is technically— *technically*—his fault, he's the nearest available outlet.

"Ha!" I say, trying—and failing—to keep my frustration in check. "How, exactly, did you *earn* a 'good night'?

By kissing me uninvited? Twice! Or by letting the entire assembly at my cousin's debut party believe we were a couple—"

"Hey, I was just following your lead on that one." He climbs off the bike and squares off with me.

"Or, wait," I say, ignoring his comment and gathering steam. "Maybe it was by spending all day flirting and holding hands with my boy-crazy cousin while I was stuck in the palace smelling like a frogging lobster." I shove against his chest with both palms. Hard. "You're right. Good." Another shove. "Night!"

I turn and stomp away, reveling in my dramatic exit. I'm almost to the front steps when he stops me with a laugh.

"You actually are jealous, aren't you?"

Jealous? *Jealous?!?* As if. That is the most ridiculous thing I've ever heard. I'm not even going to dignify that with a turnaround.

His biker boots clomp on the sidewalk behind me and my shoulders stiffen. If he touches me—

"I'm not interested in your cousin, Princess," he whispers next to my ear. "She's a child. Fun to hang with for a day, maybe, but I prefer a little more . . . depth."

For some reason, most of my temper melts away. I wasn't jealous—for the love of Poseidon, I don't *want* Quince's attention—but something about his reassurance calms me.

"The bond," I mutter.

Between the emotional mess buzzing between us and Daddy's decree and—I slump—yes, I admit, some bond-induced jealousy of Dosinia, it's no wonder I feel like I'm on a roller coaster of mood extremes.

For once, I'm not sure if I'd rather fall into a temporary peace accord or revive our regular tension. Whatever the reason, maybe because it's been a really long weekend, for tonight I just let it go.

"You'll need to drink a lot of salt water," I say softly. "Probably a few glasses a day."

A brief silence pings between us.

"Anything else?"

I resist the urge to lean back into him. The memory of how nice and strong and safe his arms—Stop! It's the bond. Thebondthebondthebond.

"Take baths," I blurt. "Every night." Then, because I'm not used to being nice to him, I add, "Ice-cold baths."

"Ice-cold?" he asks, his voice full of that ever-present humor.

"Well, maybe room temperature."

"I can do that."

"That'll get you through the week."

Another *ping* of silence.

"Thank you."

Without turning around, I walk the four steps up to my porch. As my foot touches the white-painted boards of the porch floor, Quince says, "Good night, Lily."

His heavy boots swish through the grass between our houses.

When I'm sure he's out of range, I whisper, "Good night, Quince."

14

*A*s far as Mondays go, today is pretty par for the course. I woke up late to find Prithi licking my ear, I smeared lip gloss on three different shirts before washing it all off and going bare, and I accidentally froze my orange juice into a solid block. So by the time Shannen finds me at my locker before first period, I'm about ready to slam my head in the door.

"What happened to you?" she demands.

I fling my locker door shut and then hoist my unzipped backpack over my shoulder, sending half the contents flying through the hall. My shoulders slump. After we've gathered up my textbooks and binders, I say, "What *hasn't* happened?"

"I mean at the dance," Shannen says. "You went to meet Brody in the library and never came back. What happened? How did it go? How did you get home? I tried to call, but your aunt said you went to stay with your dad for the weekend."

We fall into step on our way to class.

"Quince gave me a ride," I admit.

"Quince?" Shannen hurries in front of me and turns so she's walking backward. "Quince *Fletcher?*"

As if there are any other Quinces around.

"Uh-huh."

"On his motorcycle?"

"Uh-huh."

"Quince?" she repeats, unbelieving. *"Fletcher?"*

"Yes, Shannen," I say, exasperated. "Quince. Me. Motorcycle."

"What were you—"

"Lily!"

Speak of the devilfish.

A groan seeps from me. I know that ignoring him won't make him go away—in fact, I'm starting to think it only encourages him—but I just can't formulate a response. I was so not prepared to deal with the inevitable questions from Shannen. Especially not after the morning I've had.

"Wait up," he calls to us.

Shannen, still walking backward, looks over my shoulder—presumably at Quince hurrying to catch up.

"What's going on?" she mouths.

As if I could explain. I just kind of roll my eyes and shake my head.

"Hey," he says as he reaches my side. "You left before I

could offer you a ride to school."

"I prefer walking," I reply, avoiding Shannen's wide-eyed, questioning gaze. "A unicycle would be safer than that death trap."

Okay, maybe I shouldn't have insulted his baby. He loves that bike more than just about anything. Still, I think I underestimated his retaliation skills.

"You didn't seem to mind the death trap last night," he says smoothly, with a hint of innuendo that I know does not escape Shannen's notice.

I stop in the middle of the hallway outside my American government classroom. A stunned Shannen stumbles a few steps back before catching herself, then watches, jaw dropped, as I turn on Quince.

"Did you want something?" I demand. "Or were you just trying to make my morning even worse?"

A spark of something—pain? or maybe sympathy?—flashes in his eyes. When he opens his mouth, somehow I know he's going to apologize. *Damselfish*, this bond is making me way too in tune with his feelings.

"Forget it," I interrupt before he can speak. "I'm having a rotten morning. I didn't mean to take it out on you."

Shannen makes a kind of choking sound.

Quince steps closer and, in a low voice that doesn't carry beyond the two of us, says, "I'm sorry." (See, I was right.) "I know this whole mess doesn't change things between us." He looks down, his eyelids lowering until his dark blond lashes fan out over his beautiful eyes. "But I keep having this urge to stick close. To protect you, or something."

"I know," I whisper. "It's the bond. Magic." Then, as I remember Shannen watching from a few feet away, I hurry to add, "We can talk after school."

I rarely look into his eyes when I'm not furious with him. I feel the pull of his emotions mingling with mine and magnified by the bond. It's hypnotizing. Especially since he looks just as drawn in.

Thankfully, his gaze shifts over my shoulder to Shannen, and when he looks back at me, he's got some of that trademark attitude in place. He shakes his head. "Lunch."

Unprepared to argue, I nod. He sidesteps and disappears into the crowded hallway. I can still feel him, though.

Great white shark, I need this separation before I get totally bondwashed.

"Excuse me?" Shannen blurts, stepping up to my side. "Did I miss something? What happened Friday night? Did something go wrong with Brody in the library?"

"No," I insist. Not eager for the entire school to hear this tale, I drag Shannen into our classroom. "No, he never showed up. Quince did."

"And . . ."

I twist into my desk, dropping my bag on the floor with a defeated *thump*. "And he kissed me."

"What?" she squeals, dropping into her desk across the aisle. "Oh my God, how was it? Was he good? I bet he was good. He looks good, like he knows—"

"Shh!" I lean in close so she gets the clue to turn down the volume. "It was what it was. I'd rather forget about it."

"Then what was that in the hall just now?" she asks, observant as always. "And why were you on his bike last night?"

"It's complicated," I say. How on earth can I ever explain the situation without telling Shannen my secret? I should have been thinking about this on the swim home last night, but I was too twisted up and turned around to think about much of anything.

"What?" She leans sideways so far, I'm afraid she'll tip over. "Are you two *dating* now?"

I almost shout, *"NO!!! Omifreakingod, are you crazy?!?"*

But then I think, How else can I explain the situation? And things are only going to get worse over the next few days. The bond will continue to pull stronger every day. Since I can't just say, "When he kissed me, we were instantly joined by a magical mermaid bond that Capheira created to encourage mermate fidelity and stave off loneliness in the cold, vast ocean," this might be the only logical explanation we can offer.

Quince will just have to go along.

So, as much as it goes against my every Quince-hating principle, I hang my head and mutter, "Yeah, kind of."

I'm saved from further explanation by the bell, a pop quiz, and a notes-intensive lecture on the Bill of Rights. But the instant the dismissal bell rings, Shannen has her bag on her shoulder and her questions ready.

"How did it happen?" she asks as we pour into the hall. "Was it sweet? Did you have a date last night? Does this mean you're over Brody?"

"No!" I blurt. "No, no. Of course not."

Instead of taking notes during class, I focused on preparing my answers to the questions she was bound to ask. Not good for my flagging GPA, but a worthy sacrifice.

I've got my story all worked out. "It's kind of a misunderstanding. After he kissed me"—I ignore Shannen's sigh of envy—"I was so startled, I just kind of nodded. I didn't even realize he'd asked me out until he dropped me off at home and said he'd pick me up at seven."

"But then you told him, right?" She hitches her bag up higher on her shoulder. "Why is he still acting all possessive if you told him it was a mistake?"

"Because I, um, didn't." I hadn't considered that totally logical follow-up question. Geez, this is getting more complicated by the second. Now I remember why I usually never lie.

"Then what?" she demands. "You're, like, *actually* dating him?"

There is no easy way out of this, so I might as well dig in. "Well, kind of." At Shannen's shocked look, I add, "For a little while." Then, remembering what Quince said Friday night before we left for the dance, I get an idea. "It might make Brody jealous."

Shannen's brown eyes narrow. "You're using Quince?"

"Don't make it sound so awful." Then, because the idea of using someone like that, even someone I generally despise, makes me feel a little sick, I add, "Besides, he's kind of in on it. It was his idea." Not a lie.

"Oh." Shannen sounds disappointed. I'm not sure whether it's because I'm not using Quince, or because I'm not actually dating him. She asks, "How long do you two plan on keeping up this façade?"

"A week," I blurt. "Just a week. Then we'll break it off and be back to normal."

Quince and I can play nice for a week, right? I just need to explain to him why this cover story is necessary. He'll understand. I hope.

"Absolutely not," I tell Quince the next day after school. "I'm going to the swim meet with Shannen. You're not invited."

I slam my locker shut and turn away from the stormy look on his face.

"It's a free country," he says, falling into step beside me. "I can go if I want to."

I shrug as if I don't care, when the last thing I want is Quince at the swim meet. This is my Brody time, and I don't want the bond muddying my thinking.

"Besides," he says, shoving his hands into his back pockets so his leather jacket pulls open and his T-shirt stretches tight over his chest—not that I noticed or anything. "If we're pretending to pretend to be an item, I can't just let you go swoon over another guy for a few hours."

Swoon? Ha! I don't swoon. Get anxious and tongue-tied? Yes. But I got over the whole swooning-at-the-sight-of-him thing ages ago. Last month, I think.

"I'm not going to swoon," I insist. "I'm the team manager. I have official duties, like submitting the roster, recording the times, making sure everyone's at the starting block on time."

"Right," Quince says with complete insincerity. "So I'll be there to support you in your official capacity."

We push through the exit and out into the late-afternoon sun. Shannen's car is in the front row, and I can see that she's not in it yet. Since I'm waiting for her—driving and I are like oil and water . . . literally—I turn on Quince.

"Listen." I drop my backpack and cross my arms over my chest. "This whole fake dating thing is a cover, to explain things we just can't explain. It's not real. I'm not your girlfriend, pretend or otherwise. You don't have the right to act all jealous and possessive."

Quince steps closer. "It may be an act," he says, his voice low. How does he still smell of mint toothpaste at the end of the day? "But as far as most of Seaview High is concerned, it's the real deal. I'm not about to play the school fool while my supposed girlfriend drools over another guy."

I can feel his male pride swirling around me, wrapping

me in a cloud of possession. Even if we both know this is pretend, the bond magic is making the fake emotions feel real. Clearly, Quince can't tell the difference. Who am I kidding? *I* can't tell the difference, and I've been around this magic my entire life.

What crazy leap of logic ever led me to believe that we could pull this off without a hitch? Nothing ever goes that smoothly. Especially when magic and little white lies are involved. And clearly, Quince is using this as another opportunity to make my life miserable.

The door we just came through swings open, and from the corner of my eye I see Courtney and two of her groupies emerge. Before I can even groan, I feel Quince's arm wrap around my waist and pull me tight.

"What the—"

His mouth is on mine before I can finish my startled question. I'm too stunned to react, so I just hang there like a limp jellyfish in his arms. As Courtney and her crew pass by, I hear her say, "PDA much?"

The groupies giggle on cue. Why do all the most embarrassing moments of my life have to come with witnesses?

Quince releases me, gives me an arrogant smile, and then says, "See you at the pool."

Then he turns and saunters off toward his motorcycle. I'm staring at his retreating, leather-clad back when Shannen emerges.

"Were you and Quince just . . . kissing?"

"Yes," I say, wanting to stomp my feet at his obnoxious-ness. "That rotten sneak."

"Yeah. . . ." Shannen's voice sounds kind of dreamy. "Rotten."

"Come on." I grab my backpack and set off toward Shannen's car. "Let's get to the meet."

"This is certainly going to be an interesting week," she says, unlocking her car with the remote.

We both fling our bags into the backseat and then climb into the front. Too bad she can never know just *how* inter-esting.

Watching Brody swim the butterfly is like watching music in motion. One strong pull through the water. Head lifting for a deep breath. Arms flying forward in tandem. Diving ahead with a powerful kick.

I could watch him swim forever.

I laugh at the thought that, once I get this thing with Quince taken care of and I make things work with Brody, hopefully I *will* be watching him swim forever.

"What's so funny, princess?"

My moment of bliss vanishes. My spine stiffens and my jaw clenches.

Not only did Quince show up at the meet, but he's sitting right behind me on the bleachers. The hair on the back of my neck keeps standing up every time I sense his movement. Like I expect him to grab me or kiss my neck or something.

"Nothing," I grind out. I glance at the scoreboard to get Brody's fifty-yard split. Quickly jotting the time into the record book, I return my attention to the pool.

Brody has the lead by at least a body length. Of course, Brody always has the lead. In my three years as team manager, I've never seen him lose a race. Even at the state meet.

Shannen leans in close from my left and whispers, "Courtney at three o'clock."

Setting my feet on the bleacher in front of me, I twist my head to the right and see Brody's ex settle in with her groupies a few feet down from us. Why is she here? She and Brody broke up. She shouldn't be anywhere near the swim team.

As Brody makes his final turn in the race, Courtney jumps to her feet and cheers. "Go, Brody!"

She's not the only one, of course. Everyone in the stands is now yelling every time he takes a breath. Shouting, "Go! Go! Go!" whenever there's a chance he might hear them.

Still, I'm surprised that Courtney is cheering him on.

"Looks like she isn't ready to let her man go," Quince says, not bothering to whisper.

I throw him a scowl. Then I remember that I'm pretending he's not here, and I focus on the race. Brody touches the wall first. When his time flashes on the scoreboard, I pencil it into the record book. Flipping to the page with his best times, I compare his latest result. It's his fastest

100 fly by two-tenths of a second. At this rate he's liable to shatter the state record.

I don't have time to thrill at his success, because the 500 free race is about to start. I check the roster against the lanes to confirm that our racers are in lanes two and seven. They climb onto the blocks, our coach lifts the starting buzzer, and then the blaring horn echoes through the natatorium—why do humans need such a long word for an indoor pool?—and the racers take off.

I'm making notes about Jeff Fetzer's slow start when I sense someone standing in front of me.

I look up to see Brody, chlorinated water dripping from his dark curls and a towel wrapped around his waist, smiling expectantly at me. The smell of chlorine makes me nauseous—it's toxic but not fatal to merfolk, so I try to keep my distance from pool water—but I can handle a little tummy ache for Brody.

"So?"

I beam. "Your best time. By two-tenths."

"Awesome," Brody replies with a bigger grin, still panting from the race. Butterfly is the most exhausting of all the strokes. I tried swimming it in my terraped form once and nearly drowned. Well, figuratively. Anyway, his chest is still rising and falling with each labored breath, and his cheeks are red with the increased blood flow. It will take Brody several minutes for his vitals to return to normal. And I will enjoy watching every second of his recovery.

His attention shifts over my shoulder, and my blood chills. He sees Quince at my back. This is a major moment. Since I came up with the jealousy cover story for Shannen, the idea has been growing on me. If I'm stuck with Quince, I might as well try to get something out of it. I'm about to find out if it's going to work. What will Brody's reaction be to seeing Quince with me? Will he be happy for me? (Bad.) Or ambivalent? (Also not good.) If I'm lucky, he'll be angry or arrogant or possessive. (All signs of potential jealousy— aka very, very good.)

He doesn't get a chance to react before the blowfish says, "Nice swim, Bennett."

Brody smiles, apparently not as confused as I am by Quince's compliment. "Thanks."

Then, before I can consider what's going on, I feel Quince's leather-jacket-less arms, bare up to the muscle-hugging sleeves of his tee, wrap around my chest and shoulders. On instinct, my hands grab at his forearm, ready to pull him off, when he says, "You're lucky I'm not the jealous type, for all the attention Lily spends on you and the team."

I can feel the smile in Quince's voice, but also the knife's-edge undertone. He's warning Brody off.

"Quince—" I start to argue, but Brody cuts me off.

"Lil's a great manager," he says with an overly friendly grin. Then his eyes flick to me, and there is something . . . appraising in his look. Like he's seeing me in a new way. "We're lucky to have her."

As an experiment, I soften my hands that were ready to pull Quince off me and instead hug him tighter. Brody's eyes narrow a tiny bit. When I tilt my head against Quince's and Brody's jaw clenches, I know I'm on to something. Seeing me with Quince *is* making him jealous!

I am so excited by the thought that I relax back into Quince's chest.

"I need to go fuel up for my next race," Brody says, looking annoyed. (By my actions? Yay!) "I'll catch you later."

"Later," Quince says dismissively.

As Brody walks toward the locker room—past a furious-looking Courtney and gang—I turn to Quince.

"Did you see that?"

"See what?" Quince says, staring over my head at the long-distance race still in its first hundred.

I scowl. What's his problem?

I turn to Shannen. "Did you see that? Brody was totally jealous!"

"Yeah," she says, not as enthusiastic as I'd expected. "That's great."

Oh, well. Maybe she just feels awkward in front of Quince. We'll squee later. Turning back to the race—and realizing that I've missed the first two split times for both of our racers—I can't stop smiling.

It's not until the six-minute race is over that I realize I'm still leaning back against Quince with his arms around me. For some reason—I'm telling myself it's because he's more comfortable than the backless bleachers—I don't pull out of his embrace. Besides, the better the show we put on, the more Brody will see that he has feelings for me. It's win-win.

"$\mathcal{A}$nd congratulations to the swim team for their win last night over Parkcrest. Senior Brody Bennett set two school records and took home four blue ribbons. Come out and support the swimming Sea Turtles next Thursday at the city championship meet!"

As the video announcements continue, my mind freezes on the image of Brody holding up his blue ribbons in front of the NO RUNNING OR HORSEPLAY sign. I still can't believe Brody acted jealous over Quince. I mean, you can't be jealous over a girl you're not interested in, right?

I've never felt so hopeful about my future with Brody— and I'm only slightly annoyed that it's thanks to Quince's interference. Someday, when Brody and I are an old bonded sea couple, I might even thank the blowfish.

"Earth to Lily," Shannen says, waving her hand in front of my dazed face. "We need to talk about our history project."

"Right," I say, trying to bring myself back into the moment, into homeroom. Then Brody's news clip comes on and I tune out everything else. I know every word by heart, because I edited the piece, but it still gives me a thrill to hear his voice.

"Yearbooks will be on sale next week." He holds up the sample the yearbook staff made, flipping through the pages of pictures documenting our school year. "You can place your order during lunch and in your homeroom classes until next Friday. Be sure to reserve your piece of history before it's too late."

As he holds the book open to the page with the swim team picture, I sigh back into my seat. I will never get tired of listening to Brody. Or looking at him. Or thinking about him—

"Lily!" Shannen drops a history textbook on my desk, jarring me out of my daydreaming.

Heart racing, I look at her and then the textbook. "Right," I say, sitting up straight and opening the book to the chapter on the Fertile Crescent. "History project. I'm on it."

Shannen rolls her eyes at me but turns her desk around to face me so we can get to work. I'm proud of myself for focusing on our project—which is a report, analysis, and re-creation of one of Hammurabi's laws—for the rest of homeroom. She only has to prod me back to attention once. Or maybe twice.

When the bell dismisses us from homeroom, we head

down the hall toward the gym. I hate gym. After spending most of my life in the water, it's not like land-based coordination comes real easily to me. In fact, it's a great day when I don't walk out of gym with some kind of sports-related injury—red welts on my arms from volleyball, skinned knees from track, a lump on my head from a tennis racket. But the one shining light about gym class is that it's one of the two classes I have with Brody. Sure, it doesn't show me at my best like news team does—neither does trig, for that matter—but I'll take any time I can spend with him.

Plus Quince isn't here to get in my way.

"I think we're starting a new unit today," Shannen says as we push through the locker-room door.

"That can only be a good thing," I reply. "I don't think I would have survived another week of soccer."

We change into our gym uniforms—hideous, itchy navy blue shorts and baggy white tees with SEAVIEW in big powder blue letters across the chest. Some girls—ones with more curves than me and less baby fat than Shannen—wear tight SEAVIEW tank tops instead of the baggy tees. If I wore one of those, it would only highlight my less-than-overflowing assets.

"I don't see any equipment," Shannen whispers as we emerge into the stinky gym.

She's right. The gym looks unnaturally plain. The bleachers that usually fill either side of the basketball court have been collapsed back against the walls. The basketball goals

169

are in place, but there aren't any racks of basketballs next to our coaches, who are standing at center court with their whistles at the ready. The few kids who have beaten us into the gym are loitering along the sidelines, looking just as confused as we feel.

Shannen and I head for the padded wall at the end of the court and slide down to the floor.

"Maybe we're going outside?" she suggests.

"Usually when we do that," I say, "one of the coaches is out there waiting."

But not today. Both of our coaches—the tennis coach, Miss Bailey, who is always ultraperky, and one of the baseball coaches, Coach Pittman, who is the complete opposite of perky—are in the gym, watching us trickle through the doors.

The bell rings and the last stragglers, including Brody, wander into the gym.

Coach Pittman blows his whistle while Miss Bailey claps her hands, shouting, "Circle up, everyone."

Shannen and I reluctantly get up and move to center court, along with everyone else. I edge us as close to Brody as I can get without making it too obvious.

"Today we are going to start a unit on playground games," Miss Bailey says excitedly, as if her enthusiasm might be contagious. She ignores the fact that every last one of us groans—I don't know about anyone else, but I'm groaning because I'm clueless. "For our first game, the rules are simple.

Coach Pittman and I will select one of you to be—"

"Freeze tag," Pittman bellows over Miss Bailey's instructions. He eyes the crowd for a second before pointing at me and Brody. "Sanderson and Bennett, you're it."

Then he blows his whistle and all shellfish breaks out. Kids flee to the four corners of the room.

I'm it? I'm *it*? What does that mean?

"We've got this, Lil," Brody says.

"Got what?" I look around helplessly. "I don't even know what we're doing."

"You don't know how to play freeze tag?" he asks, incredulous. When I shake my head, he gives me a quick lesson. "When you touch someone, they'll freeze. Only someone who's not it can unfreeze them. If we freeze everyone in class, we'll win."

"Oh." I don't get it. "Okay."

Brody apparently sees my continued confusion. "Just try and touch as many people as you can."

Then he takes off, leaving me standing at center court with still no real clue about this game.

I watch him as he chases after a group of freshman girls who just giggle instead of running away. As he touches each of them, they freeze in place. Another girl, a sophomore I think, runs up and touches them, bringing them back to life. But before they can get away, Brody refreezes the freshmen and catches the sophomore, too.

"Get moving, Sanderson," Coach Pittman shouts. "Or

you'll get a no effort for the day."

That gets me running. My grades are bad enough without tanking gym. In a complete lack of strategy, I just run for the nearest bodies. They're fast, though, and escape to the other side of the gym, using some of Brody's victims as a shield. But while I'm trying to find a way around—or through—the frozen girls, Brody sneaks up from behind and freezes my prey.

"Nice teamwork, Lil," he says with a wink. And then he jerks his head to my right. I turn and spot Shannen and the junior girl we hang out with during gym sometimes. I'm starting to get the appeal of the game.

"Don't move, Shannen," I say, slowly walking toward them as they back away. "It'll be painless. I promise."

"No way." She starts to turn and run but finds herself face-to-face with Brody, who has circled around lightning fast.

"Sorry, girls." He grins as he touches each of them on the shoulder. To me, he says, "Let's get the bunch in the corner."

We set off after the rest of the class. Somehow, I feel like we're connecting over more than a game. We're bonding—a nonmagical but still awesome kind of bond. I never knew gym class could be so great.

Brody catches up with me and Shannen as we leave the gym hall, heading for the science wing (I have earth science and

Shannen has AP physics). I still feel kind of flushed from all the exertion of chasing my classmates around the gym when Brody jogs up, throws an arm around my shoulder (my backpack, actually), and says, "We make a good team, Lil."

I exchange an omigod look with Shannen.

"Yeah," I say, amazed that I'm able to form words. I mean, Brody is practically hugging me! "A great team."

He squeezes me to his side, like he would one of his swim-team buddies, but I feel little sparks everywhere our bodies connect. "We should partner up more often. No one else would stand a chance."

He's probably forgetting my incident with the jump rope and the bloody noses (plural), but I'm not about to remind him.

"Totally." I'm trying to play it cool—something I have zero experience with—because I learned my lesson about appearing overeager when I asked him to the dance last week. Look how (not) well that turned out.

As we round the corner for the science hall, I sling my arm around him to complete the buddy-buddy hug we have going. Only, the second I see Quince—or rather, the second he sees us—I know that we don't look buddy-buddy to him. His fury hits me like an emotional tidal wave. His eyes turn bright as flames, and the muscles in his jaw clench so tight, I think he might be in danger of crushing his teeth. I hope he has a good dentist.

"Lily," he grinds out without loosening his jaw. He

said my name, but his burning eyes are trained on Brody. "Bennett."

It might have been a greeting, but there are two signs that Quince is issuing a warning. First, he got Brody's last name right. Second, he didn't so much *say* the name as *growl* it.

"Hi, Quince," Shannen says, as if there's no deadly tension in the air.

"Shannen." Quince nods in her direction but doesn't take his eyes off Brody.

Brody, clearly not as oblivious as Shannen, says, "I better get to class. Winslow will dock my grade if I'm late again, and Coach will kill me if I lose my eligibility."

Then—I think he might secretly have a death wish—he winks at me before disappearing down the hall.

"Lil—"

I don't let Quince finish before I launch at him. Throwing my full body weight into it, I slam him up against the lockers. He blinks super-fast, like he's not sure what just happened.

"What is wrong with you?" I demand. "Couldn't you see I was finally making headway with—"

"Lily!" Shannen gasps.

"What?" I snap, twisting my head to face her.

She raises her eyebrows and kind of twitches her head down the hall. I see Assistant Principal Lopez talking with Shannen's physics teacher two doors away.

Holy mackerel, what am I doing? The kind of violence I'm displaying is not only totally out of character, but also grounds for immediate suspension, for sure. I'm still holding Quince against the lockers with my forearms braced on his chest (yes, I know I'm only holding him there because he's letting me). This roller coaster of emotions or hormones or bond-magic-induced moods is wearing me out. Suddenly overwhelmed by the situation and the secrecy and the emotion flooding through me, I let my head drop forward to rest on Quince's chest. For some reason—the bond—I feel better just touching him. Like all my anger seeps out of me.

Quince leans his head down next to mine and whispers, "Relax, princess. It's all part of the game, remember?"

I shake my head.

Is it a game? It's getting harder to remember the rules.

"You should tell Shannen."

I jerk back. "Tell Shannen what?"

"Tell me what?" Shannen asks at the same time.

He looks me straight in the eyes as he says, "The truth."

"I can't." Panic sets in. He can't really mean the *truth*. The only truth I've ever kept hidden from my best human friend. I try to convey with my eyes—and through the bond—how much it hurts me to keep this secret from Shannen—especially when Quince, of all people, knows the truth. I shake my head vehemently. Doesn't he realize how important the secret is? Of course not. It's not his secret.

"Then I'll tell her," he says.

"No!"

"Tell me *what?*"

"Lily is—"

"Don't!"

"—only pretending to go out with me." He gives me a wry grin. "But I'm not. I'm trying to convince her to choose me over that idiot."

I sag against him in relief. For a second I had been so sure he was going to blurt out my entire secret in the middle of the hall, where the whole school could hear. I've never been so terrified in my entire life. Not even the time a rogue shark slipped through the Thalassinian border defense.

Now, with my fears calmed, I get a feeling of longing. His words sink in. Was that part of the game too?

"Oh, that?" Shannen waves him off. "I knew *that.*"

She *knew* that?

The bell rings, sending Shannen hurrying off to her physics class, leaving me totally stunned in place.

"You know I would never reveal your secret," he says softly, more like the gentler Quince I saw in Thalassinia. "Never."

He's sincere. I can feel it. And he's a little hurt that I doubted him. Maybe he's right. I should know better. He might be rude and obnoxious and a major pain in my tail fin, but he's also honorable. He would never betray my kingdom.

I should feel major relief about that—and I do, really I do. But . . . there is a teeny tiny (guilt-ridden) part of me that secretly wishes he had done it, told Shannen the truth about me. Because then there wouldn't be this invisible wall between me and my best human friend, and I could blame someone else if it went bad.

I can't bring myself to thank him for something I almost wish he hadn't done. Instead, I focus on what led to this moment—Brody—and fall back on something far more comfortable with Quince: anger.

"Why do you have to ruin every good moment I have with him?" I push away from Quince, putting a few feet between us.

"I don't like seeing you with him," he says, sounding irritated that the conversation has returned to Brody. "It makes my blood boil just thinking about—"

"It's the bond," I insist.

Maybe Quince was still in shock when I first told him what the magic was all about. I still remember the first time Daddy gave me "the talk" about the bond. He was all awkward and uncomfortable, going on about hormones and commitment and not letting any unscrupulous merboy talk me into kissing him before I was ready. After a while, my eyes crossed, and I'm pretty sure I tuned out the last half of the conversation. So it's not a major leap to think the details could be a little murky for Quince, considering everything that got heaped onto him at once.

"That's what's making you feel jealous about Brody," I explain. "The bond connects us and amplifies our emotional reactions. It's designed to make mermates more in love."

I can't help laughing at the thought of me and Quince in love. It's such a ridiculous notion that I can't even imagine a world in which that would happen.

"I don't believe it," Quince says with absolute certainty. "I don't believe anything magical can make someone more in love."

He jams his hands into his jeans pockets and leans back against a locker, lifting one heavy biker boot to pound on the gray metal door. He looks me right in the eye as he says, "Love is already the strongest magic in the world."

The laughter drains right out of me. It's obvious that he truly believes this. He believes in the omnipotent nature of love. I never knew he was such a romantic.

But he doesn't know my world. There are magical forces he can never understand, and love is not at the top of the list.

"Quince and Lily," Mr. Lopez says, walking up to us. "You two need to get to class."

"Yes, sir," Quince replies, but doesn't move from the lockers.

Thankful for the reprieve, I turn and hurry to my earth science class. I'm so lost in thought about Quince that I barely register when my teacher says, "You're late, Lily.

You'll need two sheets of notebook paper for our pop quiz."

My mind is still out in the hall with that unexpected romantic version of Quince. Where has he been hiding the last three years?

16

*P*eri is waiting for me beneath the buoy one nautical mile out from the pier. I can tell from the look on her face that she's eager to hear all the exciting details of my first week as a bonded mermaid. She's not going to like them.

"Hey," she says, swimming over to me. "How are you—"

"I think I'm losing my mind."

"Why?" Her elegant brown brows draw together. "What happened?"

"Quince is being nice to me."

Her laugh bubbles out before she can slap her hand over her mouth. "What does that have to do with it?"

"He's never nice to me," I complain. "Rude, yes. Obnoxious, always. But never nice."

"That can't be true," she says as we swim down to the seafloor. "The boy is obviously nuts about you."

"You've got that half right," I mutter as I drag my hand through the sand, idly watching a flathead dart from his uncovered hiding place. "He's definitely nuts."

Peri twists into a sitting position and pulls her long brown waves over her shoulder. With swift, elegant fingers she deftly weaves her hair into a braid. "I think you've got blinders on, girl," she says, very matter-of-fact. "He was perfectly pleasant last weekend."

"It must be the bond." I reach back for my blond frizz— thankfully turned silken in the sea—and start a braid. "It's messing with our feelings. I'm like a frogging tidal wave of alternating emotions. And he's no better. He practically bit off my head for walking with Brody yesterday."

"You were walking with Brody?"

"Yes!" Why am I talking about Quince when I have Brody news? "Coach Pittman made us it in freeze tag, and we caught everyone in class, and then afterward—"

In my excitement, my hands get tangled in my hair. Peri swims to me, moves my hands out of the way, and takes over the braiding.

"—and then afterward he put his arm around me and said we make a great team."

I twist around to look at her, tugging my hair out of her hands. Ignoring her annoyed scowl, I say, "Isn't that great? That has to be a good sign. Right?"

"I suppose," she says, grabbing my shoulders and turning me around so she can finish my hair. "But terraped boys aren't as easy to understand as mer boys."

"Tell me about it." I think back to the afternoon of the swim meet. "I mean, one second Quince and I are arguing, and the next he's kissing me because Brody's ex is walking by. Then, at the swim meet, he's all hugging me and whispering in my ear like we're true mermates or something."

Peri gets really quiet behind me. She takes my now-perfect braid and hangs it carefully over my shoulder. I turn around to find out why she's gone silent, but then I see. A massive Portuguese man-of-war is floating by just a few feet away.

We may live at peace with most of the ocean world, but there are definite exceptions—namely, sharks, poisonous jellyfish, and killer whales (they aren't *all* Shamu). We're no more immune to jellyfish stings than humans—maybe even less so because of our delicate skin.

Without saying a word, I wrap my hand around Peri's wrist and swim as stealthily as possible in the opposite direction. Man-of-wars aren't intelligent predators, but disturbing the water around them could send their tentacles into deadly motion.

I know why Peri is petrified. When she was six, her younger brother was killed in a man-of-war attack that left her badly scarred but clinging to life. It took the palace medical staff weeks to nurse her back to health. They never could erase her scars or her nightmares.

182

When we get out of range, I place my hands on either side of her face.

"We're okay," I say reassuringly. "We're safe now."

Her eyes are wide and unseeing.

"Peri." I move my face in front of hers. "Peri, come back to me."

Slowly, gradually, I see her return to the present. I've been with her during sightings before. I don't know where she goes in that faraway look, but I always bring her back.

"I—I'm—"

"It's okay," I say, hugging her close, forcing myself not to cringe at the feel of the scars lacing across her shoulders. I see them in my mind as clearly as I've seen them with my eyes a thousand times. Dozens of thin, pearly white, almost iridescent lines crisscrossing over the copper mer mark just beneath her neck. I've always been proud of her for not hiding them. I don't know if I could ever be that unself-conscious.

When she squeezes me back, I know she's all right.

"I'm s-sorry," she stammers. "I wish I didn't go into a panic like that. Won't do me a drop of good if I freeze up in their path."

"Well," I say, trying to lighten the mood, "we just have to make sure you never face one alone. I'll always be there for you."

When she leans back, her eyes sparkle with the same copper shade as her scales.

"You know that's not possible," she says, fidgeting with

the braid still draping over my shoulder. "But I appreciate the sentiment." She gets a little bit of that far-off look again, but this time it's different. "You are such a caring mer-person, Lily. You deserve someone who will love you as much as you love your friends."

I laugh. I can't help it. Considering my current romantic mess, it's either that or cry. And if I go home with puffy red eyes—sparkling or not—Aunt Rachel will know some-thing's wrong, so I break out in the giggles.

"I'm working on that," I say. "Just as soon as Daddy separates me from the lug-nut biker boy, I'm confessing everything to Brody."

Her eyes—sparkling a little less—flash.

"Not *everything*?" she clarifies.

I hadn't really thought about it until this moment, but it's fast becoming the only option. My birthday is only five weeks away, and once he's my mermate, he'll have to know the truth anyway.

I nod.

"Lily, you can't," Peri argues. "If you tell a human who hasn't been given *aqua vide*—"

"I know. It's a risk when Brody hasn't begun the change to water life." I sigh, thinking of Brody with his arm around me, flying through the water as if he were born to it, smiling down at me from my homeroom TV screen every Monday, Wednesday, and Friday. Every thought of Brody is more per-fect than the last. "But he's worth it."

Peri doesn't look quite satisfied, but she doesn't argue. She knows as well as anyone—except maybe Shannen—how long I've loved Brody. If Quince hadn't made a mud puddle of everything, Brody might already be mine.

"I need to get home," I say, thinking of my pile of homework for tomorrow and of Peri swimming back to Thalassinia in the waning sunlight. "Will you be okay getting back?"

"I'll be fine," Peri insists.

I hug her once more, just because. "See you tomorrow night."

Hopefully, twenty-four hours from now, my bond with Quince will be a distant memory. Brody will be mine before Monday.

17

"*I*'m home, Aunt Rachel," I shout as I burst through the kitchen door after school on Friday. "I'm just going to drop off my backpack, and then Quince and I are heading for—"

I stop midsentence when I see the messenger gull sitting on our refrigerator.

Prithi is positioned in front of the fridge, tail curling slowly back and forth, silently daring the gull to leave his perch.

Aunt Rachel walks in from the hall. Nodding at the gull, she says, "He's been here for two hours. Wouldn't let me take the message."

I roll my eyes. The note isn't private, or the kelpaper around his leg would be pale pink instead of green. Messenger gulls are our primary means of communicating with our land-based and landlocked kin, but they aren't always the most reliable. This one probably read a signal wrong and thinks this is a top-secret message.

"Hey, Lily," Quince says, entering behind me without bothering to knock. "I had to get gas on the way home, but I'm ready to go." He stops when he sees the gull. "Is that a seagull on your refrigerator?"

"A messenger gull," I clarify, stepping forward to retrieve the message from the gull's leg. Prithi finally realizes I'm in the room and starts her ritual weaving around my ankles.

"Afternoon, Quince," Aunt Rachel says. "Want something to eat before you go?"

"No, thank you, ma'am," he says, pouring on some seriously unnecessary charm. "My mama always told me not to swim on a full stomach."

They share a laugh—a human joke, I imagine—as I unroll the scroll. My heart jumps. I can't help the little squeal of joy that escapes.

"What's up?" Quince asks, coming to my side and reading the note over my shoulder. "'Come to the Hideaway.' What's the Hideaway?"

"Only my favorite restaurant on the entire planet!"

Daddy must be taking us to a celebratory last supper before the separation. I'm so excited that I actually try to hug the messenger gull, who just squawks and flaps his broad wings to keep me away. This draws Prithi's attention, and she makes a grab for the bird.

As I watch Aunt Rachel and Quince try to separate them,

getting the gull out the window and Prithi into the living room, I just smile. Tonight is going to be such a huge relief.

"You're going to love it," I say as we swim up to the front door of the Hideaway.

"Why do you say that?" Quince asks.

"Because"—I push open the massive wooden door, unable to hide my grin—"they don't serve a single piece of sushi."

"Thank heavens." But he laughs as he says it.

Daddy first took me to the Hideaway for my twelfth birthday. I remember swimming through these doors for the first time, floating into a little piece of the human world under the sea. It's a salvager's paradise. The walls are covered in the rich brown deck boards of a Spanish galleon. All the tables and chairs are made from the square-cut bones of a pirate schooner. They set their tables with actual knives and forks—not a set of seasticks in sight.

But my absolute favorite part is the giant column of glass filling the center of the restaurant. Inside that column is a true piece of land, a terrarium complete with grass, a small pine tree, and—this is the absolute best part—a pair of cardinals!

I'm not sure how it works, how they get fresh air and sunshine, but it is an amazing feat of mer technology.

As we swim up to the hostess counter, Quince looks totally in awe. "Nice," he says. "Where'd they find all this stuff?"

"The seafloor." I shrug. "For centuries humans viewed the ocean as a dumping ground."

"Some of them still do," Quince says.

So true. "We just cleaned up the mess they left behind."

Before we can get into some kind of environmental discussion, the hostess swims up. "Princess Lily!" she squeals, her short parrotfish-blue hair waving around her head like a halo. "How nice to see you again!"

"Hi, Tang," I reply. "Is my father here yet?"

"He's in the captain's quarters."

"Thanks." The captain's quarters is a small private dining room in the back. Its walls are covered in the crystal drops of countless ocean-liner chandeliers, making it feel like you're eating inside a diamond or a giant geode. Daddy doesn't usually care about privacy, so I'm not sure why he's making the big gesture tonight.

"Come on," I say to Quince as I head for the room. "Let's get this separation over with."

The second we float through the crystal-beaded curtain covering the door to the captain's quarters, I know something is up. Daddy is not alone at the big round table. Graysby and Grouper are on one side of him, and Calliope Ebbsworth is on the other.

"Oh, no," I breathe.

"What?" Quince asks, swimming closer to my side. "Is something wrong?"

I just shake my head—it's not like I can throw a fit before

189

I'm a thousand percent certain of what's about to happen. But I know. Daddy's not settling for a rubber-stamped couples counseling. He's bringing out the Challenge—an archaic three-test trial to prove irreconcilability. Otherwise Calliope and his advisers wouldn't need to be here.

"Lily," Daddy says with a big smile. Then, still smiling, "Quince."

"What's going on, Daddy?" I ask, trying to sound even tempered.

As if he senses my internal freak-out, Quince's hand comes up against the small of my back. I know it's just the bond easing my emotions, but I'm thankful for the gesture.

"I asked Graysby, Grouper, and Calliope to join us for dinner," Daddy says as if nothing's going on.

"Greetings, Princess," Graysby says.

Grouper smiles. "Master Quince."

Quince nods at them.

"Calliope," I say to Quince, because I'm sure everyone else in the room already knows what's going on, "is the Thalassinian bond facilitator."

"The what?"

I close my eyes and take a deep breath. "She's a mermate couples counselor."

"It's a matter of protocol," Daddy says as the server clears the table. "According to Thalassinian law you must prove due diligence in your relationship before you can declare for a separation."

"That's a technicality and you know it," I retort. "No one has enforced due diligence in decades."

I see the change in Daddy's face, in his eyes, long before he speaks. He does not appreciate my questioning his judgment or authority in front of his subjects. "Whatever has happened in the past," he says in his royal voice, "I choose to enforce it now. You are a princess of Thalassinia and therefore subject to greater scrutiny than her citizens."

"But Daddy—"

"You are not above the law, daughter." His eyes soften and he adds, "And you are not blessed with a surplus of time."

"Is *that* what this is about?" I kick up from the table. "You think I'm going to wind up bondless on my birthday? That's why we have to go through this?"

"Go through what?" Quince asks.

Daddy does not acknowledge him. "Partly."

"I'll have you know," I rant as I swim around the table, "I *have* a mate picked out. If this blowfish hadn't messed things up by kissing me, then Brody and I might already—"

"Enough!" Daddy's echoing shout silences me. In his brook-no-dissent tone, he says, "Whatever the situation back on land, the fact is, you *are* bonded to this boy." He glances at Quince, giving him a curt nod. "You are subject to the law and my rule. You will go through the Challenge before I grant your separation." Then, just so I don't mistake his meaning, he adds, "Assuming you have proven the unsuitability of the match."

"What about Quince?" I ask, grasping at anything that might get me—us—out of this mess. "He can't just disappear for a weekend. I mean, last weekend was bad enough, that was just a day—"

"I have already sent a messenger gull to Rachel, asking her to give an explanation to his mother." Daddy gives me a stern look. "You will not get out of this Challenge."

"The Challenge?" Quince asks. "What's the Challenge?"

Calliope speaks up, finally. "It's terribly romantic, actually," she says, making swoony eyes. "You and the princess will be sent to a deserted island for the next two days, with only each other and brief visits from friends and family for company."

"Deserted?" Quince repeats. "How deserted?"

"You, me, and a palm tree," I say.

"Not even an island monkey?" he asks with a smile.

I find myself smiling back despite my anger. "Maybe a seagull or two."

"This is serious, Lily," Daddy says. "Calliope will visit you to evaluate your situation, as will I."

I release a heavy sigh as I sink back down into my seat. "I know."

If Quince and I can't prove we're an unsuitable match, Calliope has the same power Daddy has to deny the separation. I'm not sure why Daddy is doing this, but clearly we're not getting out of it. Now that it's begun, I just want to get it over with.

"How soon do we start?" I ask.

Calliope brightens. "Immediately." She gathers her massive bag from the floor. "I will be happy to show you to the island and explain the rules."

I nod. "Let's do it."

18

*T*he "island" is really a tiny atoll, a ring of sand-covered reef that peeks through the surface. At least the sand is deep enough to support some grasses and shrubby bushes and one sad palm tree that grows at a forty-five-degree angle to the ground. At the center of the ring is a blue hole, like a private plunge pool.

"The rules of the Challenge are simple," Calliope says. "For the next two days you cannot leave the bounds of the island. If you need hydration or salinization, use the blue hole."

"What about food?" Quince asks.

Leave it to a guy to focus on his stomach. We just ate!

"All necessary sustenance will be provided. You may choose to shelter on land, but I would recommend the pool." Calliope seems way too excited about this.

I guess it's not very often that she gets to perform her

full duties. Especially in the case of a mer-terraped bond. Humans in Thalassinia aren't totally unheard of; we get a few each year. But usually they are so undeniably in love with their mermate that a separation is unthinkable. My situation is unique, to say the least.

"You will be presented with three tests," she says, positively glowing with enthusiasm. "You might not know you are facing a test at the time, but your performance will still be evaluated."

"Great," I mutter.

Quince asks, "So, we pass the tests, and then the separation goes ahead?"

"They are not pass or fail," she explains. "Your performance in the Challenge is evaluated by his highness and myself. At the end of the forty-eight hours, I will make my recommendation, but the king will make the final decision."

"Fine." I kick at the sand. "Let's get started."

Calliope clucks at me—yes, actually clucks. "I'll leave you, then. Your first test will be administered in the morning."

She turns and dives into the sea, transfiguring from her finkini to her fin as she sails through the air. Great. I drop down onto the sand. The last thing I wanted this weekend was to be stuck on a stupid island with Quince. We were supposed to be separated by now. I'd been thinking, We'll have dinner, then the separation, and maybe frozen sugar cakes for dessert. Not, We'll spend two days together on a stupid island.

I need to get back to Brody.

Quince lowers onto the sand next to me.

"I know you're pissed," he says, staring out at the ocean horizon. "I can feel it. But we'll get through this, and then it'll be over."

He doesn't sound quite as eager for the separation as I feel, but he must want to get this over and done so he can get back to his regular life. A weekend on a deserted island wasn't exactly in his plans, either.

"Even though it's partly your fault," I say, although there's not a lot of accusation behind my words—he didn't know the mess he'd be getting into with that kiss—"I'm sorry you got dragged into this whole thing. My dad is taking it kind of disproportionately serious."

"No big," he says with a shrug. "I mean, it's not every day a guy gets to hang in a magical, mythical kingdom surrounded by beautiful mermaids."

He leans into me, nudging me with his shoulder. Like a buddy.

Yeah, right. Beautiful. Not me. No one has ever looked at me and thought, Wow, that Lily Sanderson is one beautiful girl. On my best day, I'm cute. On my worst, a frizz-balled mess.

"You're being hard on yourself, aren't you?" Quince asks.

"What do you mean?"

"I don't know for sure," he says, rubbing his wrists on his knees. "I just get the feeling that you're thinking negatively about yourself. I know that sounds ridiculous—"

"No," I interrupt. "It doesn't. The emotional connection of the bond gets stronger the longer it goes on."

"Oh." He turns to look at me. "So you *were* being hard on yourself?"

I can't see any reason to lie. "I guess so."

"Why?"

"I just—" I feel kind of ridiculous talking to Quince, of all people, about this. With the bond connecting us, though, he'll probably understand better than anyone right now. "I know I'm not beautiful. Underwater I feel almost pretty, but on land . . ." I hold out my already-frizzed hair as evidence. "I feel like a mess."

"You don't think you're beautiful?" His voice is low and uninflected.

"I know I'm not," I reply. "Not like Courtney or Dosinia. Even Peri has an elegant kind of beauty. I'm just . . . me."

Me, with the freckles and skinny legs and too-big lips and eyes. Who could find that attractive? I'm like a speckled ostrich.

"You shouldn't make assumptions about how others view you, Lily." He sounds so sincere, I can't help but look up as he adds, "Some people find beauty in chaos."

Without waiting for a response, he pushes to his feet and walks away. As I stare at his retreating back, I ask, "Hey, was that from a poem or something?"

Just before he jumps into the pool, he says, "Or something."

I sit on the beach—staring after him and kind of wondering what the shellfish is going on—until the evening chill hits me. With the sun sinking below the horizon, the surface temperature drops a dozen degrees. Time to turn in for the night—at least I can warm the water in the pool to a decent temp. Tomorrow will bring the tests. As soon as Daddy and Calliope realize Quince and I are the worst match in merworld history, we'll be separated and back home before you can say "Some people find beauty in chaos."

Now, why did that phrase stick with me?

"Morning, sleepyheads."

Peri's voice penetrates my deep fog of sleep. What is Peri doing in my bedroom? She's never visited Aunt Rachel's house.

"Aren't you two just as cozy as a pair of pearls in a puka shell?"

I bolt upright at the sound of Dosinia's sneering comment. I *know* Doe is not in my room—she hates the human world and wouldn't set foot on the mainland if you paid her.

The first thing I remember is I'm not in my room. I'm in

the deep blue hole on Calliope's Challenge island. And the second thing is that I fell asleep next to Quince so my temperature regulation would keep him warm too.

Only sometime in the night we moved from sleeping *next* to each other to sleeping *cuddled* together.

Roused from his sleep by my movements, he stretches his arms wide and yawns so loud, he practically roars. "Morning, princess."

Peri clears her throat with a pointed *a-hem*.

Quince's eyes finally spread open. His broad smile shows no shame—not that we have anything to be ashamed about. "Morning, ladies. What brings you to our fair island?"

"The Challenge," Peri replies with a smile. "I'm administering one of your tests."

With a strong kick, I jet away from his side. Giving Dosinia a skeptical look, I ask, "And why are you here?"

She shrugs and purses her glossy lips. "Uncle Whelk asked me to help."

Thanks, Daddy.

Certain I look like a fright, I try to tame my curls by running fingers through my hair. It's so unfair that Quince can wake up looking exactly like he did when he went to sleep, only with sleepy eyes and pink cheeks.

"So what's the test?" I ask Peri, trying to ignore how Dosinia is eyeballing Quince's bare chest. Maybe I should have made him keep the T-shirt on this time.

"It's going to be super-cool," Peri exclaims. "You're each going to make a gift for the other."

"A gift?" I ask.

"Yes." She claps her hands. "I'll stay in the pool and help you create your gift. Dosinia will go with Quince above the surface to make his."

"Are there any requirements?" Quince asks, proving that he's actually awake and paying attention.

"Nope." Peri shakes her head. "Just that it has to be hand-made. And with Lily in mind."

This sounds dumb. How does my making a gift for Quince prove anything about our unsuitability?

He doesn't seem quite as skeptical. "Let's get to it."

With a strong push off the ledge that has been our bed, he shoots toward the surface. Dosinia looks right at me as she says, "This should be fun." Then she smirks and follows Quince.

"Could she be any more obnoxious?" I ask once she breaks the surface.

"Probably," Peri says absently. "So what do you want to make?"

I look around the hole. All I see is a reef wall dotted with brightly colored anemones and sea fans and other marine life. If this gift is supposed to be for Quince, I can't use anything perishable like anemones or kelp. On land, those would just rot in a day or two and wind up making his room stink worse than it probably already does.

"I have no idea, Per," I complain. "The hole doesn't have much to offer."

"Why don't we explore some?" she suggests. "I'll go up, you go down."

I shrug in agreement. As she kicks up to the top of the hole, I swim down. This is stupid. I'm never going to find something that Quince will—

Before I even finish my mental whine, I see it. A perfect blue sand dollar, about an inch and a half across. Quince was fascinated by the sculpture in the starfish room, so maybe he'll like this.

I let Peri know I've found something. Her shadow moves over me as she swims down to inspect my find.

Maybe I'm wrong.

"He's going to hate it," I grumble. "I don't know anything about what he'd want. See, we're totally unsuitable."

"You never know," Peri says, admiring the sand dollar. "Maybe he'll love it."

I shrug off her suggestion. It doesn't matter. I'm not about to spend all day making a stupid gift for a stupid test because my dad won't grant the stupid separation. Quickly locating some *chorda*, I braid together a makeshift string that I know will dry into a ropelike finish when it hits the air. In a few minutes, I've finished the cord and strung the sand dollar at the center.

To seal the blue color, I hold the sand dollar between my palms and flash-freeze it.

"What do you think?" I ask, holding it up for Peri to inspect. I'm actually pretty proud of my creation.

"I think," she says, eyeing the necklace and then me, "that I don't understand why you hate him so much."

I scowl. Where did that come from? I tie the necklace around my neck so I don't lose it.

"I don't hate him," I admit. "Not really. Sometimes I think I do, but he's not really an awful guy *all* the time."

"So what then?" Peri swims up and studies my face. "Why throw away a perfectly good bond?"

A perfectly good bond? I'm not sure what's going on here. I mean, Peri is on my side. Isn't she? She knows how I feel about Brody. Why is she encouraging me to keep Quince— as if he's mine to keep anyway?

"You know why," I say, my water-dulled frustration coming out as mild annoyance.

"Brody," she says, sounding disappointed.

"Yes," I reply. "Brody. The guy I've been in love with for three years. The guy I'm *supposed* to be bonded with."

"Don't get defensive." Peri waves her tail fin back and forth in an agitated gesture. "I just don't understand why Brody is so much more appealing than Quince. Explain it to me."

"Quince is . . ." I whip around in a circle, trying to gather my thoughts. "He's everything I don't want. He's rude and pushy and loves tweaking me at every opportunity. He is a land lover with two capital Ls." I stop spinning and try to face Peri, but the world around me keeps whirling for several seconds. "Did you know he couldn't even swim before last weekend?"

"So?" Peri argues. "Now he can."

"You don't get it," I complain. "I belong in the water. Brody belongs here too." I take a breath, picturing Brody swimming the butterfly. And then Quince on his disaster of a motorcycle. "Quince belongs on land."

Peri studies my face, my eyes, like she's trying to read my deepest thoughts. If anyone can, it's her. But I don't get to find out what she sees. In the end, she gives me a gentle smile. "I'm sure everything will work out how it's supposed to."

Yeah, with me and Brody together under the sea, while Quince stays safe and permanently dry, where he belongs.

"I hope so," I say as we begin our ascent. "I desperately hope so."

As we break the surface, I don't see Quince and Dosinia anywhere. Which is troubling, because Calliope said we couldn't leave the bounds of the island. If Dosinia tricked Quince into breaking the rules, I'll strangle her. The last thing I need is this Challenge voided so we have to start over or something.

Then I hear giggling from beyond the shrubby bushes on the north side of the island.

"You are so good with your hands," Doe coos in her boy-hunting sultry voice. "I can't think of a merman in Thalassinia with that kind of skill."

Quince's low laughter carries, though I can't hear his response.

With a growl, I launch myself up onto the sand, transfiguring into my finkini on the fly. She doesn't even *like* humans. Does she have to flirt with every boy with a pulse? I mean, is she too oblivious to see that this is kind of a delicate situation? Can't she put the flirt on pause just this once?

No, I don't suppose she can.

"Dosinia!" I snap as I stomp through the grass in the direction of her voice. "What are you—"

But when I reach the clearing of the sandy beach, I am stunned speechless by what I see. Quince and Dosinia are sitting side by side, shoulder to shoulder, facing the beach. At my shout, they both turn to face me. Dosinia, now facing his back, wraps her arms around his waist and hugs herself along his spine.

He doesn't even react.

"Took you long enough," she says with a sneer. "Quincy's been done for ages. I've been . . . *entertaining* him."

Quincy? My eyebrows shoot up . . . and then dive into a scowl. Before I know what I'm doing, I stalk up to them, grab Doe by the arm, and yank her to her feet.

"Get out of here!" I give her a push toward the water. "You're not part of this test. No one's making *you* stay inside island lines. Go home."

Quince, who has scrambled to his feet by the time I'm done, catches Doe before she stumbles to the ground.

"What the hell, Lily?" he demands.

I feel tears filling my eyes, and I don't even know why. The bond is messing with my emotions so much, I can't think straight.

Dosinia, who has never known when to back down, sneers and says, "If you want him to yourself, then why don't you stay bonded?"

"What?" I glare at her. "This isn't about him," I insist. "It's about you. About how you always take such joy in making my life miserable."

I turn, prepared to stomp away, but then turn back. "You know what? The two of you have that in common."

Then I run through the grass to the other side of the island. It's not nearly far enough away. As soon as I clear the grass, I drop to the sand. Wrapping my arms around my knees, I let my head slump and I try to use deep breathing to keep my tears away.

What is the matter with me? I never used to be this emotional. I never used to lose my temper or yell at anyone—well, no one but Quince. Now I feel like I'm snapping at everyone.

The grass behind me swooshes with the sound of someone walking. I fully expect it to be Peri, my best friend, come to calm me down. No one else knows me well enough.

But the feet I see through my tear-blurred eyes do not have Peri's pretty, copper-tipped toes. They're big, bare masculine feet.

I huff out a sigh.

"That was a little harsh," he says as he lowers himself to the sand at my side.

I gaze up at the sky. "I know."

"She's jealous of you."

"Who?" I ask, scowling. "Dosinia? Not likely."

Quince makes a noise that sounds half like a laugh and half like a growl. "Sometimes you can be so blind when it comes to people, princess."

Like he knows anything? He's known Doe for a week— and barely that. I almost point that out . . . but something about his off-the-wall statement rings true.

"What would she have to be jealous of?" I demand. "She's the pretty one. The flirty one. The one all the boys chase after."

He gives me a half smile. "Not *all* the boys."

"Don't flatter yourself," I say. "She's been awful to me since long before you showed up."

"Lily," he says, his tone serious, "you're the princess. The golden child. The entire kingdom looks to you for their future. She's just . . . your little cousin. Second string."

I never thought of it that way. All I ever knew was how jealous I am of her, of her anonymity and her easy way with boys and her classic beauty. She's everything I'm not. I never thought she might have something to be jealous of, too. I never thought I was worth anyone's jealousy.

"Just food for thought," Quince says, pushing back to his

feet. He extends his hand, inviting me to take it. "Now let's go back and exchange gifts so we can get to the next part of this Challenge."

As I slip my small, pale, freckled hand into his big, tan one, I wonder how it happened that the boy who always made my life so miserable could now make me feel so calm. For the first time, I start to think that Quince and I might wind up friends.

Long after Peri and Dosinia have gone, Quince and I sit on the beach where we traded gifts. He looked happy enough with the necklace—the smile he gave me might have been the first genuine one we've shared—but it was nothing compared to his gift for me.

"I can't believe you had time to do all this," I repeat, sounding like a broken record. It's a small miracle. I shake my head. "How did you learn to do this?"

On the beach before us, just beyond the reach of high tide, is a massive sand castle. But this is not just any sand castle with uneven walls and bucket-shaped turrets. No, this is an almost-perfect scale replica of the Thalassinian royal palace. Complete down to the curtains on my bedroom window.

Quince shrugs, like it's no big deal, but I can feel his pride at my obvious pleasure. "My dad used to take me to the beach a lot. He liked to build sand castles, so I got plenty of practice."

I don't know much about Quince's dad other than the fact that he's not around. I think Quince sees him once a year. I can't imagine having a living parent not be part of your life. If would kill me if Mom were alive and just . . . absent.

But maybe it's better than nothing.

"Your dad," I begin, suddenly interested in learning more about Quince's life. "Where does he——"

"The necklace is great," Quince says abruptly, as if that's the logical next moment in our conversation, and not a diversion tactic—which it obviously is.

I almost call him on it, forcing him to at least listen to my question. Until I see the faraway look in his eyes . . . and feel the underlying pain.

I'm not that cruel.

"Compared to your castle," I say instead, "my necklace looks like a cheap tourist trinket."

"No," Quince insists, his mood lightening. He lifts the sand dollar from his chest and studies its cinquefoil design. "It's perfect. One of a kind. You can't even take my gift home."

"I have a mental photograph." I flash him a smile. "I'll remember it every time I see the real thing."

When I say that, his gaze shifts out over the ocean, to the horizon, like he can see all the way back to the mainland. The air falls silent, even the breeze stills, and I feel a surprising sadness—whether it's his or mine I'm not sure.

208

I expect him to say something—I'm not sure what, though I'm almost eager to hear it—but he just kind of sighs and gives me a lopsided smile.

Something urges me to fill the silence. "You know—"

"There you are, darlings," Calliope's singsong voice trills. "I thought you might have left."

We both turn to see her walking toward us from the other side of the island.

"No, ma'am," Quince says politely, rising to his feet and holding down a hand to me. "Wouldn't want to violate the rules of the Challenge."

Judging from the blissful look on her face, I can see that is just the right thing to say to her. "Excellent," she coos. "Excellent."

I let him pull me to my feet, standing and dusting the sand off the back of my finkini.

"How was your first test?" she asks. Then, noticing the sand sculpture behind us, says, "Ooh, Lily, that is a perfect replica of your palace. What a wonderful gift for Quince."

"Actually, ma'am," Quince says, ducking his head as his cheeks turn an adorably dusky shade of pink, "that was my gift to Lily."

"Oh," she says, her eyes wide. "Oh, my."

Feeling left out—and completely outshined by Quince's gift—I reach over and slip my hand beneath his sand-dollar pendant. "This was my gift."

Calliope walks closer and leans in to inspect. "It's beautiful, my dear." She smiles up at me. "Just beautiful."

"Yeah," Quince agrees. "It is."

Calliope steps back and studies us for a moment. I have a bad feeling about the suspicious look in her eyes. But then she just smiles and says, "Time for my test. Let's move to the western shore so we can watch the sun set."

A minute later, she's arranged us on the sand, Quince and me sitting cross-legged and facing each other, with Calliope to one side between us.

"Let me first explain the rules of my test." She pulls a clipboard out of the satchel she's brought with her, flips to a specific page, and then reads aloud. "During the execution of the I Say, You Say test, participants must remain facing each other, they must maintain eye contact while making each proclamation, and they must continue until the Challenge administrator deems the test complete." She lifts her eyes from the page long enough to ask, "Understood?"

We both nod, although I'm sure Quince is as clueless as I am.

"Excellent." She sets down the clipboard. "Now here is what we're going to do. First, I would like each of you to say three positive things about the other. It may be a compliment or an encouragement or just something you like or admire."

Panic tightens around my throat. I'm pretty sure it's because I'm afraid I won't have any nice things to say about

Quince. But a tiny part of me says it's because I'm worried he won't have any nice things to say about me.

I've always been pretty awful to him.

"Now, let's see." Calliope studies us once again. "Who should go first?"

Not me, not me, not me, not—

"Lily," Calliope finally declares. "Why don't you start us off? Say something positive about Quince."

"I, uh . . ." Words won't come. My brain freezes. My eyes lock on Quince's, and I block out the anticipation I sense he's feeling. I hate being put on the spot, even if it's only two pairs of eyes waiting for my next move. Finally, out of desperation, I blurt the first thing that comes to mind. "He has pretty eyes."

Those pretty eyes crinkle at the corners, and I heave a sigh of relief. If he's smiling, then I must have said something right.

"Very good, Lily," Calliope says, "but I'd like you to use his name when you make your statement. Don't anonymize him with a generic pronoun."

That sounds a little like psychological hooey, but when I look back at him and say, "Quince has pretty eyes," I feel it in my gut.

Calliope's psychological hooey has some teeth.

"Wonderful," she says. Then, to Quince, "Your turn."

Quince doesn't hesitate for a second. "Lily is fiercely loyal."

I jerk back, stunned. Am I? I guess I never really thought about it, but I do stand up for my own. I might not defend myself all the time, but I'll throw down with anyone who says a word against Peri or Shannen, or Daddy or Aunt Rachel. I'm more than a little surprised that Quince noticed.

"Perfect." Calliope nods at me. "Your turn."

I'm still reeling a little from his comment, but I try to focus enough to come up with something less . . . superficial than my first. For some reason, I think back to that moment in the bathroom stall after he stopped me from going after Courtney for making fun of Shannen. How he held me tight and reassured me. I take a deep breath and try not to think before I say, "Quince can be very tender."

He winks at me.

Then, before Calliope can cheer my statement or tell him to go, he says, "Lily has no sense of fashion."

"Hey," I cry. "You're supposed to say something *nice*."

"No arguing, Lily," Calliope chides. "This is not a dialogue."

But Quince ignores her, keeping his gaze locked on mine, and says, "That *was* nice. I can't stand trend chasers and wannabe supermodels. I like girls who are fresh and unique. Individual. Like you."

Calling someone unique isn't always a positive, but the way Quince says it makes it sound like a huge compliment. I kinda like the idea of being fresh and unique. Makes me sound like an exotic flower.

I'm picturing myself as a bird-of-paradise when Calliope says, "Your turn, Lily."

Oh, right. My turn. The test, Lily, the test. I try to rein in my floral fantasy and return to the task of figuring out what I like about Quince.

No one seems in a rush to hurry me up, so I have time to compose my thoughts. I try to distance myself from the situation and look at him with my fresh and unique eyes. He's sitting there, watching me, as if we're alone on the island. Calliope could be in the South Pacific for all he cares.

That gives me an idea.

I take a deep breath before finally saying, "Quince doesn't care what others think of him."

That's the biggest compliment I can give someone. I mean, I can't *stop* worrying about what others think of me. Boy, do I wish I could have that kind of carefree confidence. I just don't have it in me.

He looks like he wants to respond, to say something about my compliment. I can feel a conflicting emotion in him. Some mix of pride and frustration and anger. I'm confused. Why would my comment make him angry?

Like I'm compelled to defend myself, I say, "I just meant that you—"

"I care." The anger is there, an undertone in his voice. An intensity in his eyes. "Sometimes I think I care too much."

His gaze falls away, shifting to the ground between us

while he drags one finger in a swirling pattern through the sand.

"Eye contact," Calliope chides. "Quince, it's your turn."

He doesn't react immediately. For several long seconds he keeps making spiral designs with his finger. When he looks back up, the anger is gone, wiped away with one shutter of his thick-lashed lids. "Lily doesn't think before she speaks."

Grrr. I do think. I just sometimes think things I shouldn't say out loud.

"Wonderful," Calliope says, making notes on her clipboard. "Now we can—"

"Hey," I complain, "we were supposed to say positive things. I bought your 'no fashion sense' argument, but how was that last thing a compliment?"

"Lily, you shouldn't judge—"

"You don't have a filter," Quince interrupts. "You're honest, sometimes to a fault, and straightforward. Too many people say what they think others want to hear."

I scowl, still not certain that was praise.

But apparently Calliope isn't as doubtful. "Excellent." She's practically clapping. "Let's move on to the second part of this exercise."

Great. The first part went so well, I can hardly wait for the second.

"Now that we've established things you admire about each other," she says, "it's time to address the other side. I would like each of you to share one thing you would change about the other person. Try to make it a positive criticism instead of an attack. If you like, you might also touch on how you can help them achieve that change."

Well, at least this will be easy. I have a list as long as the Bimini Road of things I'd like to change about Quince.

"Quince," she says, "why don't you go first this time?"

All the hairs on the back of my neck stand up. If all of his "compliments" sounded suspiciously like criticisms, I'm almost afraid to hear an actual criticism.

"If I could change one thing about Lily," he begins. Then he's quiet for several long seconds, like he has to think really hard about what he's going to say. Just when I'm debating whether this is because he has too many things to choose from or because he can't think of anything he'd want to change, he says, "I'd want her to see beneath the surface of the people around her."

What does he mean by that? What does he know about how I see other people? I see all the way down to his depths. And Shannen's. And Bro— Oh. That's it. This all goes back to the Brody thing.

Figures.

"Is this about Brody?" I demand, already certain of the answer.

Calliope hushes me. "Explore that, Quince," she says. "Why do you think that needs to change?"

He kind of groans before quietly saying, "Sometimes I think Lily is too . . . self-involved to see more than—"

"Excuse me?"

"—what she wants to see."

"Self-involved? Self-involved?!?" I jump to my feet, unable to sit still. "Let's talk about *self-involved*, Mr. Kissing Unsuspecting Girls in Libraries."

"Lily, please," Calliope says. "Sit down so we can discuss this rationally."

"I didn't mean it like that, Lily," Quince says—and don't think him using my actual name is going to calm me down this time—as he stands up to face me. "It's just that you've been so caught up in Brody for so long and . . ." He runs his sandy fingers through his hair. "You don't really know him. You're in love with an image. And honestly, it's a little . . ."

My body stills. There's something ominous in the way his sentence trails off. And *honestly*, I'm itching for whatever that brings. "What, Quince?" I demand. "It's a little what?"

He groans again, jamming his hands into his back pockets before looking me straight in the eyes as he says, "Shallow."

For a good ten seconds my mind is completely blank. No coherent thoughts form—it's like I'm a jumble of words and feelings and . . . pain. That's what comes next, an overwhelming pain. This is worse, even, than when Brody turned me down for the dance. A thousand times worse.

"Lily, I—"

"No," I say, stopping the apology I know is coming. I don't want to hear it. "It's fine."

Calliope clears her throat. "Lily? Would you—"

"You want to know the one thing I would change about Quince?" A feeling of empty calm washes through me. "The fact that he's bonded to me."

He doesn't have to say anything for me to know he's feeling the same pain his words inflicted on me. I should be glad for that—it's why I said what I said. But instead I just feel . . . nothing.

Calliope stands and, very businesslike, starts gathering her belongings. "I think I've seen enough."

Good. I hope she's seen how totally unsuitable we are.

"There is a basket of food for your dinner in the blue pool," she says as she stuffs her papers and notes and clipboards into her satchel. "I believe your father will be coming in the afternoon tomorrow to administer the final test."

"All right," I say. Even though I haven't done anything but make a necklace and talk about Quince today, I feel completely drained. (He has that effect on people.) More than physically. Emotionally.

"Good night," she says, waving at us before turning and diving into the sea.

For several long minutes after she's gone, we just stand there, silent on the beach as the sun sinks into the horizon. Which is fine with me. I don't think there's anything left to say.

Quince apparently doesn't agree.

"Can I explain?"

"I don't think there's anything to explain," I reply.

"There is," he insists, stepping into my line of sight. "I know what I said hurt you, and that's the last thing I want."

"Then why?" I feel tears threatening, but I quickly tamp them down.

"I'm not sure," he says, not exactly reassuring me. "It's just that . . . there are so many things I like about you. Your generous heart and crooked smile and zillions of freckles." He lifts his hand, like he wants to touch those freckles, but drops it back to his side. "How you always smell like lime and coconut. The list could go on forever. What I said . . . that was the *only* thing I could think of that I wish was different."

Five minutes ago I didn't think there was a thing in the world that would change how I feel about Quince. But he did it. While I have an endless list of things I'd change about him, he has an endless list of things he likes about me. And only one thing he doesn't.

How can he make me go from being so mad at him that I could breathe fire, to making me feel completely rotten for even thinking that?

Yet another thing about him that completely puzzles me.

"Let's eat," I say, because I'm suddenly famished and a basket of food is way more appealing than continuing this conversation.

"Sure," Quince says, uncertain, but trying to sound upbeat. "I'm so hungry, I could even eat sushi."

I laugh. Partly at his joke, but partly at the ridiculousness of this situation. I mean, how did I—Thalassinian royal princess—wind up bonded to a land lover who can't swim and hates sushi? If ever there was a more unsuitable match, I haven't seen one. Daddy has to realize that, and if the first two test results don't convince him, then I'll just have to make sure the third does.

I follow Quince toward our dinner. By this time tomorrow, we'll be back in Seaview with this whole experience behind us.

19

*A*fter we've finished off the dinner basket—fresh uni and unagi sushi for me, grilled tuna steaks for Quince—I'm not tired at all. The sushi has revived me and, somehow, cleared my mind. Enough to know that I *don't* want to talk about all those things Quince said. Enough to know a dangerous subject when I hear one.

Rather than sink to the depths of the blue hole in a quest for sleep, I kick up to the surface and lie out on the sand, staring at the night sky above. So many twinkling points of light. All the mer technology in the sea can't re-create their delicate beauty.

Quince follows, lying at my side with his arms folded behind his head.

For several minutes neither of us says a word. Like we're just content to lie next to each other and stare at the stars. Then, before I know I'm going to do it, I break the silence.

"All the stuff you said you like about me . . . how did you know all that?"

I feel him tense. I sense every muscle in his body tighten, like a flight response, before he forces himself to relax. It's the bond, I know, giving me this insight. That doesn't make it any less alluring to be able to tap into someone else's emotions.

"I don't know," he finally says on a big exhale. "I guess I was paying attention."

"I . . ." What do you say to something like that? "I didn't know."

"Well, either I didn't want you to know"—he shifts, rolling over onto his side to face me—"or you didn't want to know."

Fighting the urge to roll onto my side, which would bring us uncomfortably face-to-face, I say, "What is that supposed to mean?"

"It means you have been too caught up in chasing your dream guy to see much of anything else."

"That's not fair." I roll to my side before I think better of it. "I love Brody. Why should I notice whether my pervy next-door neighbor has been watching me? Shouldn't the person you love come before everything else?"

Quince's eyes look accusingly into mine. "You only *think* you love Brody." He digs a hand through the sand between us, like he needs a physical outlet. "Love isn't about obsession. Love is about . . . connection."

"Obsession?" I gasp. "I'm not obsessed. I mean, not any more than any other girl in love."

"Right," he says as he rolls away from me, onto his back.

"Besides," I say, scooting forward so I can poke him in the shoulder, "what would you know about love?"

When he laughs, a self-mocking kind of laugh, I know I'm about to be in big trouble.

"Oh, Lily," he says, shaking his head. "I know about love. I know about wanting and dreaming and wishing with every piece of your soul. I know enough to recognize the difference between the parts that are real and the parts that are only in my fantasy."

He turns his head slightly to face me, and I find myself saying, "L-like what?"

"Like when she cries and my heart tears into little shreds, and all I can think of is making her forget the source of her sadness." His face is blank, emotionless. His words—and the underlying emotion bombarding me through the bond— more than make up for it. "That's real."

My voice is barely a whisper when I ask, "And fantasy?"

"Believing she might ever feel the same way."

When he swings into a sitting position, I have to stop myself from reaching for him. My hand itches to wrap around his biceps and pull him back down and . . . I don't know what. But that would sweep me into a totally different current, one I'm not prepared to drift with.

I lie there, staring at his broad back, just visible in the starlight.

"I think I'll sleep on land tonight," he says, pushing to his feet.

I feel helplessly glued to the ground, unable to make myself move or speak or do anything at all.

He pauses, like he's waiting for me to respond. Then, when I don't, he adds, "I'll be under the palm if you need me."

"Quince," I call out. I'm not sure what I want to say, but I have to say something. I scramble to my feet and gather my courage. "Why didn't you ever tell her? This girl you love. Why didn't you tell her how you feel?"

His shoulders tighten and then relax. He does that a lot. Lets the tension take over and then releases it. That must be how he always remains so calm, why I can never set him off like he does to me. He doesn't fight the emotion, he just processes it.

"Because"—his voice is heavy with a kind of resigned sadness—"she doesn't want to know."

That's the moment that I know, for certain, that he's talking about me. I might have speculated and wondered and imagined, but when he says that, I know with unwavering certainty that the "she" he's talking about is me.

And I feel like the biggest coward in history for letting him walk away.

* * *

Sometime just before daybreak I finally fall asleep. I spent hours tossing and turning and twisting in the still waters of the blue hole before finally succumbing to exhaustion on the ledge Quince and I shared the night before. So I've been asleep only an hour or two at the most when I feel someone rock me awake.

"Lily," Quince says, his hushed voice full of tension, "wake up."

I blink into the dawn light filtering through the water. "What?"

"Shh." He holds a finger to his lips, then waves a hurry-up gesture at me before kicking into the depths of the hole.

Still dazed by sleep, I follow. When I reach the seafloor, I ask, "What's going—"

But he wraps a hand over my mouth before I can finish. Then, before I have the nerve to bite him, a shadow passes above.

A human shadow.

"Oh, no," I whisper. "What are they doing here?"

"Fishing," he says. "Their engine woke me up. I watched them long enough to see they were set up with fishing gear, not diving. We should be safe down here." He glances up nervously. "At least until the sun moves directly overhead."

He's right. As long as the sunlight streaming through the water comes at an angle, there will be shadows for us to hide in. But by noon we'll be in direct view through the crystal-clear water to anyone looking.

224

"Maybe they're morning fishermen," I say. "Maybe they'll move on soon."

Besides, it's not like the blue hole is teeming with fish. Most forms of sea life are smart enough to know that a contained pool of water is not a safe place to hang out. And the isolation means they could get into the pool only during extremely high tides and severe storms.

"Guess we're stuck here for a while," Quince says, hugging the wall.

"Yeah, guess so." Something about his distance—it's emotional and physical—brings back memories of last night. "Look, Quince, about last night—"

"Forget it," he says before I can finish. "We both said a lot of things we wouldn't normally say. Let's just chalk it up to a long, emotional day. Okay?"

"Oh." I'm not sure why I'm disappointed. "Okay."

I try to tell myself it's the bond, that the warm emotions I'm feeling toward Quince are nothing more than a magic trick. But they sure feel real.

I'll have to sort them out . . . as soon as we're *not* in danger of discovery.

We settle in along the wall, waiting for the shadows above to disappear.

Two hours later, I'm starting to get nervous. I mean, what if they don't leave before noon? What if they see one of us? I would be hard enough to explain, with a green and gold tail fin for my lower body, but what about a human boy who's been underwater for two hours? That opens a whole other can of worms.

As if reading my thoughts, Quince says, "We have to do something. We can't just sit here waiting for the last few inches of shadow to disappear."

"Agreed," I say. "But what?"

"I'm not sure." He rubs his temples, like he's been thinking hard with no results. "We have to get their attention away from the hole, but I don't know how to do that when we're stuck in here."

"If only we could get to the sea," I say. "We could create some kind of diversion to make them want to leave."

"But they'd see us," he says. "It's not like we can just pop up on the surface unseen. It's clear as day up there."

"We need to mask their vision for a few seconds." I try to imagine what could conceal us from sight. "Just long enough to make a dash for it."

"Yeah," Quince says with a laugh. "We could use a thick fog bank right about now."

Thick fog. That reminds me of something Daddy taught me when I was a little girl, a just-in-case defense mechanism for situations like this.

"You're a genius!" I squeal, flinging my arms around his neck. "A fog bank."

"What?" he asks, leaning back. "You got a weather report you wanna share?"

"No, silly." For the first time in a while, I feel like I have the upper hand between us. "I *am* the weather report."

He scowls in confusion, but I don't have time to explain. The sun is rising fast and taking our shadows with it.

"Listen, I can alter the surface temperature of the water enough to make a thick fog. It won't last long. Ten seconds, maybe fifteen."

"That's okay," he says. "That's plenty of time. Then what?"

"Well, I think the only thing that will send fishermen to different waters," I explain, "is the promise of a bigger fish."

"And that fish would be . . ."

"Me."

"Absolutely not," he replies. "I won't take the chance that they'll see you. Or, God forbid"—he winces—"*catch* you."

I see the real terror in his eyes. His implacable calm is finally gone, and I'm too focused on alleviating his fears to even enjoy the moment. But I've outwitted fishermen dozens of times before. They're probably sun blind and half drunk by now, anyway. Placing my palm against his cheek, I do my best to reassure him. "They'll never see more than my fin."

He struggles for a minute, torn between what I think is his trust in me and his desire to protect me. It's scary how good I'm getting at sensing his emotions. Too bad that insight will end with the separation.

He finally covers my hand with his. "Tell me what to do."

"Stay here."

"Are you kidding?" he demands. "I'm not letting you go out there alone and risk your life——"

"I'll be careful," I insist. When he looks like he's going to protest more, I add, "You'll only get in my way."

I know that comment hurt. He likes to be the rescuer, the white knight. The thought of being helpless must be completely foreign to a guy as capable as Quince. But this is one situation where he has to let someone else save the day.

When he doesn't immediately agree, I ask, "Trust me?"

He takes a deep breath and nods.

Then, before we can say more—or change our minds—I swim up to the edge of the shadow and focus on the surface water. If I can cool it to below the dew point, it should create a sudden bank of fog above the pool that will spread out over the island. Like I said, it won't last. But it should be just enough.

I focus all my energy on chilling the water above.

When the sunlight turns from clear golden beams into blurry gray light, I make my move. As I break the surface in terraped form on the opposite side from the fishermen, I hear one of them say, "Where the hell did this come from?"

I don't stop until I reach the shore, diving and transfiguring simultaneously. Then, kicking as fast as my fins can move me—because I'm certain that once the fog has cleared, they'll be peering down into the hole and maybe spying the human-shaped outline at the bottom—I swim for their boat. It's the longest thirty seconds of my life.

Peeking around the bow of their boat, I see them standing in the dissipating fog and starting to step toward the hole. I slap my fin against the water, making a splash loud enough to be heard across the island. It works. Both men—ridiculously dressed in baggy shorts and brightly colored floral shirts (and Courtney thinks *I* have no fashion sense!)—turn at the sound. I swim out from their boat a short distance before curling into a dive, flicking my tail fin above the surface as I go. As soon as I sink to the bottom, I freeze. Muffled through the water, I hear one man say, "Did you see that one?"

"No way," the other cheers. "That's a record breaker for sure."

I move a little farther out and do my fin-slapping dive again. One more big splash, and then I hear their engine start up.

It's working!

As their boat takes off in my direction, I swim quickly, fitting in a couple more dives for show. Then, when I'm satisfied that they're far enough from the island for our safety, I sink to the bottom and watch them speed by.

I wait there for a few minutes, just to make sure I don't draw their attention back in this direction, before returning to the island. I swim to the far side, putting as much grass and brush between me and the fishing boat as possible.

Now that the threat is gone, I'm left with the aftereffects of an adrenaline rush and racing thoughts of what *might* have happened.

When I get onto land, my legs are shaking so hard, I can barely keep upright. At the pool's edge, I fall more than dive in.

Quince's arms are around me before I can fully transfigure.

"You're all right?" he demands. "They didn't see you?"

"No," I manage between terror-induced pants. "It went perfectly."

As if he's not content to trust my statement, Quince releases me and checks me over. Making sure there isn't a hook in my fin or something.

"I did it," I gasp, still reeling from the thrill and the fear. "I really—"

Quince's mouth is on mine in an instant.

His arms are around my waist, mine around his neck. It's the fear, I know it's the fear. And the bond. And the adrenaline. That whole I-was-this-close-to-death-and-am-really-really-*really*-glad-to-be-alive emotional response. Anxiety and relief and joy swirl between us until I can't tell which are his and which are mine. I can't *not* be kissing him right now.

The urgency in his kiss tells me he feels the same.

But before my body can begin to calm, another shadow

moves above us. And stays.

My heart nearly explodes in my chest.

"Well, well, well," Daddy's voice says from above. "I think this Challenge is over."

Oh, no! I jerk back and stare wide-eyed at Quince. His mouth is just as red and swollen as mine probably is. I can't even hope that Daddy didn't see what just happened because the evidence is still visible. And all I can think is, *Oh, no.*

"Daddy," I gasp, putting as much distance between myself and Quince as possible. "I thought you weren't coming until afternoon."

He levels an unreadable look at me. "It *is* afternoon."

"Oh," I mouth.

Daddy turns his gaze on Quince, who doesn't even have the decency to look embarrassed. Instead, Quince straightens his spine and says, "My apologies, sir. Your highness."

Some sort of patronizing male look passes between them, and I feel like throwing a giant conch at his head. At both their heads.

"It was a mistake," I hurry to explain. "See, there was this fishing boat, and we were trapped, and I made fog—just like you taught me—and then I ran back, and my legs nearly gave out, and then Quince was there." I cast an accusing glance his way, certain that he is somehow to blame. A slow, deep breath brings my crazed babbling into check. "Our emotions were heightened by the prospect of getting caught. It was panic." They are both looking at me with identical blank faces. "Nothing more."

Goodness knows I wouldn't knowingly kiss Quince for any other reason.

Right?

I have a feeling that last thought read clear as day across my face because Quince drops his gaze and then swims for the surface. I shouldn't feel bad—everything I said was the truth—but part of me wants to go after him and apologize. I feel rotten for hurting him.

"Lily," Daddy says, swimming down to me.

I turn away from the surface to look at him. Like a deflated life raft, I feel all my anxiety and the rush seep away. "It was a mistake, Daddy," I explain calmly. "Just a mistake."

Wasn't it?

"Was it?" Daddy asks, echoing my own question. But rather than sounding regal and authoritative, he sounds just as confused as I am. "Was it all really a mistake, Lily? All of it?"

"Of course," I say. But it is a whispered protest.

"At first, I thought maybe—" He shakes his head, showing uncharacteristic uncertainty. "But now, after this weekend . . . and the last . . ."

"Nothing's changed, Daddy." I swim closer, trying to plead with my eyes. "I promise."

"I know. It's just that I can't help feeling that you're not seeing things clearly. All the signs are there and—" Then, as if he just realized the funniest thing, he laughs. He pulls me into a gentle hug. "Oh, how I wish your mother were here," he says. "She was far better equipped on the subject of relationships."

Though I want to insist that Mom would see that this bond was ridiculous, a small part of me refuses to speak for her. I never even met her. How could I begin to know what she would say?

"Let me have a few minutes to speak with Quince," he says. "He should have a voice in all of this as well."

As Daddy swims up to the surface, to ask Quince for his opinion—great, now I feel guiltily for never having taken that into consideration—I float over to the pool wall. I can just imagine what they're saying. Daddy will ask Quince what he wants to do, and Quince will confess some sort of ridiculous undying feelings for me, and Daddy will declare it a match made in heaven. But who knows? Maybe I'm holding too high an opinion of myself. Maybe Quince doesn't want to be shackled to a mermaid anyway. Maybe he doesn't want to be doomed to spend the rest of his life in whatever form I'm currently manifesting—soon to be almost exclusively mer—which is what will happen if the bond is formalized.

Did I even tell him about that little problem? No, because I never thought it would be an issue. I never thought we'd be in a position where the bond becoming permanent was even a remote possibility. Well, I need to tell him now so he knows what he'd be giving up.

Energized, I kick to the surface. As I burst into the air,

transfiguring on the way and hoping to bring Quince over to my side of the argument, I hear Daddy say, "One week, son. I give you one week to change her mind."

"No!" I shout, landing feetfirst on the sand and running at them. "No, we have to tell Quince about the form sharing, about how if the bond isn't severed, he and I would always have to be in the same physical form, and once I return to take my place in court, I'll rarely use my terraped—"

"I know."

"What?" I snap my head at Quince. "You know what?"

"About the rules," he says with a shrug. "About being stuck in the sea whenever you are."

See, "stuck." He doesn't want to be a merman.

"Then why not end it now?" I demand, shoving against his shoulders with all my strength. "Are you insane?"

He looks at me with unwavering intensity. "Probably."

"Daddy, you have to explain—"

"One week," Daddy says. "You can wait one more week. I want you to be absolutely certain about what you want. At that time you will give me your final decision, by which I will abide." He doesn't look happy about that. "If you choose to separate, I will perform the ceremony on the new moon next weekend. That timing will make the break cleaner, in any case."

Then, as I stand there, jaw dropped and unable to comprehend how this could be happening—again!—Daddy gives me a hug, kisses the top of my head, and then disappears into the sea.

It takes several long moments for my astonishment to process into anger. Into raw fury. At Quince.

"You!" I roar. "I— This— We—" When no words come, I have no choice but to scream. *"Aaargh!"*

This can*not* be happening.

20

I don't speak to Quince on the swim back to Seaview. Or the ride back to our street. Or when I leave him in his driveway.

But when he follows me into the kitchen, all the thoughts and words and accusations bubbling inside me finally burst out.

"What did you tell him?" I demand.

"Lily—"

"You told him you were moon-eyed over me, didn't you?" I accuse. "That you have loved me from afar for three years and you can't stand the thought of being apart?"

"Now, that's not fair—"

"Lily," Aunt Rachel calls from upstairs, "is that you, dear?"

"Yes!" I shout up. Then, to Quince, "What did you tell him?"

He looks furious, standing there in front of the refrigerator with his jaw clenching and unclenching, his hands fisted at his sides, his biceps bulging and unbulging. I almost laugh. This is the first time I've ever seen him really, truly angry. It makes me feel kind of giddy.

"I told him the truth," he says simply.

I cross my arms over my chest. "And what exactly is the truth?" I retort. "It's getting so hard to keep it all straight."

"I told him," Quince says, stepping toward me, "that you can't stand me."

Why does that make my heart twist for a second? Maybe because it's not entirely true. And not entirely fair. But I'm not prepared to admit either of those things.

Holy crab cakes, this bond stuff is confusing and complicated.

I prod. "And . . ."

"And that I——"

"How was your trip?" Aunt Rachel sweeps into the room, right behind Prithi, who takes up a position at my feet. "Did the separation go smoothly?"

I almost growl in frustration. Not because Quince was about to make his first actual, true confession of his feelings—I don't care about that, remember?—but because . . . well, just because. "It didn't *go* at all."

"I don't understand," she says, pulling out one of the kitchen-table chairs and sitting down. "I thought you were going to sever the bond?"

"It's a long story, Aunt Rachel." Too long, too much for

me right now. A sudden headache pounds against my forehead, right between my eyes. I pinch the bridge of my nose between my fingers, hoping to massage it away. Prithi purrs against my ankle, as if trying to help. "I can't deal with this anymore tonight."

Not that Quince takes the hint.

"Lily, I—"

"I'm taking a bath," I announce. "I'd like you to be gone when I get out."

I don't wait to see if he looks hurt or upset or annoyed or angry. I'm all of the above, so he might as well be, too. At least a cool key lime salt bath will ease away some of my *grrr*.

The water is almost ready, with pristine white bubbles piling up to the rim of the tub, when Aunt Rachel knocks on the door.

"Are you all right, dear?" she asks in that maternal voice she gets when she's really worried about me.

I always wonder if it's the same voice my mother would have used.

"I'm fine, Aunt Rachel." I sit on the edge of the tub and lean down to drag my hand through the water, letting its calming energy soak into my skin. "It's just . . . it's been a hard week."

The door creaks open, and Prithi hurries in before Aunt Rachel sticks her head through the opening. While Prithi drags her sandpaper tongue across my toes, Aunt Rachel steps inside and leans back against the doorjamb.

"Want to talk about it?" she asks.

"I don't," I say, but then can't help adding, "I'm just so confused. I mean, I've loved Brody for . . . ever, almost as long as I've hated Quince. And I thought the blowfish hated me, too. But now it seems like maybe he doesn't hate me, maybe he even"—I try not to gag on the words—"*loves* me. It could never work, I know that. But he won't accept that. He convinced Daddy to give it another week, although Daddy was kind of wavering anyway because he wants me to figure out what I really want." As if I don't know. "And now I'm stuck bonded to Quince until *next* weekend, when I've only got five weeks until my birthday. Only five weeks left to make Brody fall enough in love with me to commit to the bond, or lose my claim to the throne permanently."

There. I've said it all. *All.*

I suck in a lungful of air and let it out, feeling my anxiety whooshing out with the heavy breath. Somehow, even though I haven't done anything but spill my guts, I feel a million times better. Like I just gave half my burden to Aunt Rachel. I hope she doesn't mind.

She smiles and hugs her arms around her waist, her rainbow-hued peasant skirt flowing out beneath her like a ruffled cake.

"Sounds like you know what you want to do."

"I do," I insist. "I want to get through this week, go

239

through the separation, and bond with Brody as quickly as possible." It sounds so simple. Three easy steps. "Then I'll never have to talk to Quince again."

"Is that what you really want?"

I don't even hesitate. "Of course."

But then the doubts come. The memories of the moments over the last few days where Quince was almost bearable. (Okay, more than bearable.) When he was kind and thoughtful and concerned and even nice. When he didn't act like it was his mission to make me furious. When he seemed like he might be an actual friend.

Those moments, though, were too far apart. Too late.

"Well, then," Aunt Rachel says, pushing away and speaking in a tone that means she might be humoring me, "I hope you get what you want."

Me too, I think as she leaves me alone with my bath. Me too.

"Meow," Prithi says.

At least she agrees with me.

I quickly strip down and sink into my bathwater. I'm just finishing my transfiguration when the phone rings.

"I'll get it!" I shout. "It's probably Shannen." I told her I'd be home Sunday night, so she's probably calling to find out how my visit with my dad went. Of course, she thinks my dad lives in Fort Lauderdale.

"Hey, Shan," I say, jabbing the phone into the cradle of my neck. "I was just going to—"

"It's not Shannen."

Omigod.

Omigodomigodomigod.

My heart bursts into a speed that even key lime salt water can't calm.

"Brody?"

"Hey, Lil," he says, his voice that honey-smooth texture that I haven't heard since Friday. "Do you have a minute?"

I have a lifetime.

Okay, I don't say that. I don't even really *think* of saying that. But I feel it.

"Sure," I say, trying to act cool—as if that's even a remote possibility for me. "What's up?"

Besides my heart rate.

"I had a question about our trig homework." He laughs nervously—Brody? Nervous? "Actually," he says, "that was my lame-ass excuse for calling. I just wanted to talk to you."

It's a major miracle—and because of the iron grip I have on the phone—that I don't drop the receiver into the water. My first thought is, *Why?* Why, after all these years, is he suddenly calling me now? But then I shake off the doubts. Who am I to question my good fortune—especially after the week I've had? Especially when Quince is nowhere around to mess things up.

Calm down, Lily. Just because he wants to talk to you doesn't mean he wants to *talk* to you. Act. Cool.

"Oh," I say, curling my tail fin nonchalantly. "What about?"

He hesitates before saying, "About the dance last week. About you asking me and me . . . saying no."

"Oh?" I'm not capable of more than that single syllable at this point.

"I just wanted you to know that"—*beep-beep*—"I regret it. Saying no, I mean."

Beep-beep.

"Um," I manage. "Can you hold for a sec? I have another call."

Beep-beep.

"Sure."

I click over, thankful for the time to gather my thoughts and knowing that Shannen will help me calm down and figure out what to say in this situation.

"Hey, Shan," I say. "You'll never guess—"

"It's not Shannen."

Son of a swordfish. Why is this happening to me? I mean, every time I'm about to get somewhere with Brody—*every time!*—he has to go and stick his big blond nose into it. Well, you know what I mean.

"What?" I snap. "I can't talk to you right now. I have—"

"I just wanted to apologize," he interrupts. "I'm sorry for how things are turning out."

"Fine," I say, eager to get him off the phone. "You've apologized. Good-bye."

"Wait!" It's the desperation in his voice that stops me from clicking back to Brody. He waits long enough to hear that I'm still there before saying, "I wish things hadn't gone this way. I wish I'd done it right. From the beginning."

I sigh and sink back against the tub. "I do too." Then, because I'm not completely taken by his charming side, "But that's not exactly an option at this point."

"I know."

"Listen, I have Brody on the other line." Is that the sound of his teeth grinding? "We can talk tomorrow, okay?"

"Okay." He sounds resigned. Until he adds, "You know, Lily, I don't think he's good enough for you."

"And you are?" I snap back.

"No," he says. "I'm not."

Then the line goes dead. Why don't I ever get to have the last word? Whatever. It doesn't matter anyway. I've got Brody—my *real* future—waiting on the other line. I don't care what a motorcycle-riding, land-loving, leather-wearing biker boy has to say about the situation.

I click back over.

"Hey, Brody," I say. "Sorry that took so long, I—"

The honking wail of a dead phone line cuts off my apology.

I slam the receiver back on the base, wondering, yet again, how Quince manages to ruin everything.

In trig on Monday, Mr. Kingsley pairs us up to work on tangents. In some great grand scheme of fate or luck or both, I get paired with Brody.

Quince gets stuck with Tiffany (aka Courtney-in-training).

Finally, an entire class period of uninterrupted—except by Kingsley's occasional lectures and reprimands—one-on-one time for me and Brody.

"Sorry about the—"

"Sorry I had to—"

We laugh, together, since we've spoken at the same time.

He smiles and says, "You first."

"I just wanted to say sorry I was gone so long on the phone last night." I glance at the offending interrupter, who—although bent over the textbook with Tiffany and seemingly intent on his work—is somehow watching me without looking at me. He's reading about tangents, but I just know that he's focused on me. Thank you, bond. "I couldn't get rid of the person on the other end."

"That's funny," Brody says, leaning over our paired desks. His right arm brushes against mine. "I was going to apologize for having to hang up. I had to go help with the dishes or Dad was going to ground me for a month."

I force a laugh, but all I can really think about is the way the soft, curly hairs of his forearm are tickling across my skin. It's the most intimate touch we've ever shared, to be sure. A sensation of warmth floods me, from my heart outward. My cheeks heat up and I feel—

I look up and find Quince's eyes burning a hole in me.

244

He would. He just *would* ruin this moment for me by doing nothing more than *look* at me.

Fine. I can play dirty, too.

"So, Brody," I say, leaning closer, making certain Quince sees me rest my fingers on Brody's wrist. "What else were you going to say last night?"

I have to suppress my glee when I see Quince's muscles tighten, one by one, starting with his jaw and moving over his shoulders and down his arms. It makes me feel powerful to know that I can make him so . . . jealous.

Ha! All this time, I've been using Quince to make Brody jealous, and it turns out I'm making Quince jealous in the process. Bonus.

"I wanted to ask you a question," Brody says.

"Ask me now."

His beautiful golden-brown eyes look directly into mine, and he asks, "Are you and Fletcher really an item?"

"Are we—" My jaw clenches. I do *not* want to be talking about Quince right now. Not when Brody and I are *finally* having an extended moment. So, rather than create a bigger mess of things, I simply say, "No. We're not."

That charade is definitely over. I'm done with playing the pretend fake girlfriend.

Brody leans back—away from me—and smiles. "Good." He folds his arms behind his head. "Because you shouldn't waste your time on that loser."

My eyes flick to said loser, who is resolutely pretending

to focus on his work. Emphasis on the pretending part.

I'm not sure why, but Brody's comment irritates me. Quince may be many things—blowfish, biker boy, rude, obnoxious, arrogant—but he's not a loser. Just because he's not a news anchor or a swim star doesn't make him a worthless member of the student body.

Wait a second. Why am I sitting here defending Quince? (Even if it was only mentally.)

"We'd better get to work," I say, pulling out my textbook and opening to our assigned page. "We've wasted half the class."

As we begin wasting the other half hurrying to finish all the work problems, my mind can't focus on math—as if it ever can—and keeps thinking about Brody. And not the usual crush-fantasy-come-true thoughts, either. No, I keep wondering why he's suddenly showing an interest. Why now, of all times? Is it because seeing me with Quince made him realize he has feelings for me? Or is this not about me at all? When the bell finally rings, Brody hurries off, saying he'll see me at the after-school news-team shoot.

I'm still zipping my backpack closed when I sense *his* presence at my side.

I pretend he's not there.

"You and your *partner* get your work done?" he asks. The question is simple, but his tone isn't.

"Yes," I say, hitching my backpack up on my shoulder and

pushing to my feet. Quince is standing right there, so I end up face-to-face—or, since he's got a few inches on me, face-to-chest.

"Move," I insist, accompanied by a shove.

"What?" he asks, his voice mockingly light. "Problem in paradise?"

"No," I snap. "Everything is just perfect."

I push harder, finally moving him out of the way. But before I can get to the door, he moves in front of me, blocking my exit.

Rather than waste my breath, I just scowl.

"You're a fool, you know," he says, sounding all superior and condescending. "You're not his type."

"Oh, yeah?" I try to sound amused, but he's definitely hit on a sensitive spot. Like I haven't worried about that exact thing for the last three years. "Then how come he called me last night? Why is he paying attention to me and flirting with me?"

Although part of me just wanted to throw that in Quince's face, another (skeptical) part of me wants to see if he confirms my doubts about Brody's sudden turnaround.

"Because," Quince says, leaning forward until I step back, "he's a little boy who doesn't like other people playing with his toys."

"His toys?" I gasp. I've never wanted to slap someone more in my life. "How dare you? I'm not his toy!"

Quince snorts. "You might as well have been. And now

that I'm on the playing field, he has to up his participation in the game so he doesn't lose you to me."

"Lose me to—" I feel my fragile control dissolving and clench my fists to stem the tide of fury. I might need an extra-long bath tonight to ease away all this anger. "You think this is about *you*? I never knew you were so self-centered. You're just jealous."

He doesn't deny my claim. He doesn't say anything at all as he stares down at me with a kind of questioning look in his eyes. Then, when I almost can't stand it anymore, he finally says, "He'll never accept you. Not after you tell him the truth."

"You're wrong," I insist, keeping my voice low so no one overhears. "He will. When he learns that I belong in the water just like he does."

"God," Quince roars, "you are so delusional! He's a shallow, small-minded, popularity-obsessed jackass who will see you as a freak rather than a treasure."

I feel every derogatory word as a slap in the face.

"You're wrong," I repeat through clenched teeth, as much for myself as for Quince. "He has depths you could never imagine. As soon as I tell him, we'll—"

"Why haven't you?"

I blink at his interruption. "What?"

"Why haven't you told him already?" He steps back, finally giving me some breathing room, and slips his hands into his back pockets. "If you've loved him so goddamn much for the last three years, why haven't you told him?"

"Because I—"

"Because you know the truth," he says, again not letting me finish. "You haven't told him—about yourself or your feelings—because deep in your soul you know that it will mean the end of your fantasy."

He turns to walk away, out of the classroom and into the hall, but the fury welling up in me at his ridiculous statement bursts out. "You'll see! I'm going to tell him and he'll fall head over heels and we'll be bonded before Daddy can finish the last line of the separation ritual!"

He doesn't stop, doesn't look back, just waves his hand back over his shoulder and says, "I'll believe it when I see it."

Aaargh! He makes me so flip-flopping furious. I'll show him. I'll tell Brody and he'll think it's the coolest thing ever, and he'll confess to secret feelings for me, too. I'll be done with Quince and ready to move on with my future. With Brody. In Thalassinia.

I'll tell him. After the city championship on Thursday night.

What could be more perfect?

21

*T*he week that I thought would drag on forever—like the time Peri and I sat outside Daddy's office waiting for our punishment for sneaking away to spend a day on Paradise Island—actually races by faster than I could imagine. Before I know it, I'm sitting on the bleachers in the natatorium, swim-team record book open across my lap, watching Brody swim for the city championship.

I'm still committed to the idea of telling Brody, as the adrenaline racing through my veins can attest. I'm both terrified and thrilled and, to be honest, totally nauseous. But there's no time like the present, and—not that I'd admit this to *him*—Quince was right. I've put off going after my dream for too long.

"You seem kinda stressed," Shannen says. "Something wrong?"

Unable to look away from the pool, I start to say, "No,

I—" But something stops me. I'm about to tell Brody the whole truth, but what about Shannen? She's my best human friend. It feels kind of wrong to tell Brody when she doesn't know. If I can't tell my best friend, then how on earth can I tell my future mermate?

Besides, it'll be good practice.

Handing the record book over to the freshman towel girl, I stand. "Can we talk outside for a second?"

Shannen looks confused but follows me with a shrug. We slip out the back door—passing by Quince, who's busy skulking in the back row of the bleachers—to the steps overlooking the parking lot. The night air is cool with the ocean breeze whistling through the palm fronds above.

I take a deep, calming breath.

"Shannen, I have something to tell you." I step down into the parking lot, wrapping my arms tightly around my waist so I won't spend the entire confession fidgeting. Shannen sinks onto the bottom step, and I walk over and sit next to her so I can whisper. "This is something I've never told another soul." Then I have a mental wince. "Except Quince."

But that almost doesn't count, because I didn't really have a choice.

"Okay . . ." She sounds a little dubious, like maybe I'm too much of an open book to have any juicy secrets.

Boy, will she be surprised.

"Before I came to Seaview," I explain, squeezing my arms tighter around my waist, "I didn't live in Fort Lauderdale."

Aunt Rachel and I came up with that cover story when I first moved in with her. We thought it would be easier to use something as close to the truth as possible—and we couldn't just say Daddy was dead, because, well, first of all, that just *feels* wrong, but also because I might let it slip that I was going to visit him or something, and that would be really awkward to explain.

"Oh," she says. Then she gets this kind of appalled look on her face. "You're not from the panhandle, are you?"

A little laugh escapes. "No, I'm not from the panhandle." I take a deep breath, close my eyes, and say, "I'm from Thalassinia."

"Where's that?" she asks. "Georgia?"

"It's about forty-five miles east of here."

"East?" she repeats, confused. I can tell from her tone that it doesn't make sense. "But the only thing forty-five miles east of Seaview is . . ."

"Ocean." Ready to deal with her shock, I turn to her and say, "Thalassinia is a mer kingdom. I'm a mermaid."

She looks out over the parking lot, eyes narrowed like she's putting puzzle pieces together in her head. Shannen's a brainiac, so I can bet that she's getting a pretty complete picture. Pursing her lips in consideration, she says, "You're a mermaid."

"Uh-huh."

Then her brown eyes turn on me, evaluating me head to

toe as if she might have missed some scales or gills or something.

"Well, that makes sense," she finally says. "You do have an obsession with ocean-related terminology. Though I am surprised by your affinity for sushi. I thought mermaids were supposed to be friends with fishes."

"Only in animated movies," I say with a laugh. Leave it to Shannen to intellectualize the fact that I'm a mythical creature.

She falls silent, studying the pavement. This is when the worry first hits me. What if she's flipping out? What if she thinks I'm some kind of freak of nature and she never wants to talk to me again? I might have just lost my best human friend by telling her the truth about me. And if Shannen, who's been like a sister for three years, can't see past my mer side, then how on earth will Brody? What if Quince is right, and Brody will never—

"You didn't trust me," she finally says, stopping my snowballing mental freak-out.

"Of course I did," I insist. "I do! That's why I told you."

"But you didn't," she replies. "Not until tonight." The look of hurt in her warm eyes makes me want to cry. "Why? Why didn't you tell me? And why did you tell me now?"

"I wanted to, Shan," I insist. "Oh, how I wanted to. But we have to be so careful about revealing ourselves to humans. The laws are insanely strict. There were some incidents, back in the eighteenth century, when the sea was swarming with pirates. Our world nearly made front-page headlines." I take her hand and give it a reassuring squeeze. "I trust you, but the safety of my entire kingdom comes first."

"Then why are you telling me now?" she asks.

"Because . . . I had to tell you before I——" The fear creeps up my throat again, but I swallow around it. Why am I suddenly, after three years of waiting for tonight, so full of doubts and fears? "Before I tell Brody."

"You're going to tell him?" she gasps. "Tonight?"

I nod, expecting her to squeal with excitement. To be proud of me for finally—*finally!*—taking action.

Instead, she looks worried.

"Are you sure?" she asks. "You trust him that much? You trust him with your kingdom's safety?"

All the air whooshes out of my lungs. She's just voiced the same nagging doubts I'm trying to ignore. Do I trust him? Part of me, the part that's mooned after him for three years, is screaming Yes. The rest of me, the part that knows all that mooning happened from afar with very limited personal experience, quietly whispers No.

And it's not like I can take the confession back—at least, not without an unpleasant mindwashing ritual.

"Maybe," I say, voicing my confusion. "Maybe you're right. I can't let Quince goad me into doing something stupid. This is more important than showing him up. I won't tell Brody I'm a mermaid, but I *will* tell him that I love him."

254

But . . . that didn't even sound right. It doesn't feel right to call what I feel for Brody love. That's just too—

"No freakin' way, Lil. You're a mermaid?"

Oh, no! I feel my eyes bug out at the sound of Brody's voice. I didn't hear the door open behind us—I was too focused on Shannen and her deep questions.

"Omigod," she whispers, so softly I almost don't hear. I give her a pleading, panicked look, but all she can offer in return is wide-eyed sympathy. "I think," she says, pushing to her feet, "I'll leave you two alone for a minute."

I pop to my feet at her side, willing her not to go.

She leans close and whispers, "I'll be right inside if you need me." Then she jogs up the steps and disappears through the gray metal door.

My stomach takes a dive toward my feet. It's in this instant, this moment of total fear, that I realize how wrong I was about Brody. How—Quince was right—delusional I've been. I've been living in a fantasy world, where Brody was safely removed from reality. Only in my imagination was he the perfect mate for me. If that fantasy were real, I wouldn't be so utterly terrified right now.

"Brody, I—"

"That is the coolest thing ever," he exclaims, eyeing my body as he descends to ground level. His gaze lingers over my cha-chas. "Do you wear coconut shells?"

My first reaction is revulsion. I mean, sure, there are *some* mermaids who wear things like skimpy shell bikini tops—*cough*, Dosinia, *cough*—but it's not exactly tasteful attire. My second reaction is extreme disappointment. He heard me confess my feelings—or at least what I believed were my feelings—and he obviously didn't care about that at all. He doesn't care about *me*.

And now he knows my kingdom's secret.

I have to take care of him. (No, not in a Mafia kind of way—remember, merfolk are peaceful people.) And if I can do it without resorting to a mindwashing ritual, then all the better. Because, seriously, the last thing I need right now is a weeklong killer migraine.

Forgetting my terror and embarrassment and humiliation, I burst out laughing, trying to joke it off. "You thought I was serious?" I giggle like this is the funniest thing in the world. "I was teasing. I was playing a joke on Shannen."

At first Brody looks confused, like he's not sure how he might have misinterpreted the situation. Then he shakes his head with a smile. "Nice try, Lil," he says, crossing his arms over his chest. "You wouldn't play your best friend like that. You're too nice."

It's amazing how much your life can change in just a moment. An hour ago, I would have died to be in this position with Brody, close enough to feel him breathing, and with his attention fully focused on me and him finally knowing all my secrets. But now? I've never been so scared—for myself, for my kingdom—in my entire life. Not even when

I had to lure those fishermen away from Quince.

Quince! My mind flashes back to the moment on the beach when I told him the truth, when he threw back his head and laughed. There was no fear, no humiliation, just a little relief at finally telling *someone* my secret. Who'd have thought two weeks ago that I'd be terrified because Brody found out but fine with Quince knowing?

My subconscious must have known he was trustworthy all along.

As if I'd conjured him with magic, the door above swings open and Quince is filling the doorway with his leather-jacket-clad self.

I practically sag with relief . . . until I sense the fury pounding through his blood. He felt my fear and now he's here to protect me. By any means.

That can't end well for anyone.

"Something going on I should know about?" he demands, not moving from the landing. Even though Quince makes no move, Brody steps back. "You bothering my girl, Bennett?"

"Your girl?" Brody echoes. "Not according to her."

"I lied. I am his," I blurt, desperate to keep this awful situation from going tsunami on me. Then, looking at Quince, I say, "And he's mine."

Even though I never thought it before, the moment I say it, I know it's true. It's been building and bubbling since the night he first kissed me. Maybe before.

"Does he know you're half fish?" Brody asks me. Then,

turning to Quince, he says, "You know your girl's a—"

He doesn't have time to finish before Quince's fist connects with his jaw. I'm not sure how Quince made it down the steps so fast—goodness knows he's got a corner on the laid-back-lazy market—but one second he was in the doorway, and the next he's pummeling Brody into the pavement.

Bright lights swing across the scene. Brakes squeal against the blacktop. Shannen's car stops in front of the scuffle, and the passenger door flies open.

"Come on, Lily!" she shouts. "Let's get out of here."

I stare at Quince, who has Brody pinned to the ground and held motionless beneath his knees. Quince looks at me and nods. "Go home." He bounces Brody's head against the concrete. "I'll meet you there later."

I'm tempted to nod, to let Quince beat the living carp out of Brody so I don't have to deal with the consequences of my accidental revelation. But if this whole bond fiasco has taught me anything, it's that I need to start taking control of my life. I'm almost eighteen, almost an adult in my world and in this one. I can't let someone else solve my problems for me.

"No!" I shout, diving onto Quince's back. "This isn't going to fix anything!"

Quince lets me drag him off Brody. "It's sure making me feel a hell of a lot better."

"I know." Because I felt his rush of satisfaction when his

fist connected with Brody's face. "But unless you're planning on killing him—"

"I might."

I release my grip on his shoulders. "No, you're not."

"He shouldn't know," Quince says.

Brody, who is moaning into a sitting position and wiping the trail of blood trickling from the side of his mouth, grumbles, "Damn, Fletcher. What's your glitch?"

Quince ignores him. "He can't be trusted to keep your secret."

My heart tightens when he says *your* secret. As if it's not his secret, too.

But I don't have time to explore that feeling right now.

"I know," I repeat. "Pulverizing him won't change that." Even though I know he hates feeling helpless, I have to add, "Nothing you can do will make him forget."

Quince shrugs his jacket back into place. Then, as if my words finally hit home, he asks quietly, "But you can?"

As I nod, his brows drop into a worried scowl.

I feel compelled to reassure him. "I would never use this on you," I explain. "I don't need to."

Because I trust you.

I don't have to read his mind to know that he gets my subtext.

"You need to be gone first," I say. Things will be hard enough to explain without Quince's bloody knuckles raising even more questions. "I'll be fine."

Quince nods, walking around Brody and past Shannen's still-running car, to where his motorcycle is parked next to the natatorium wall. Seconds later, his bike roars to life with a rumble that is becoming one of my favorite sounds.

"Brody," I begin once the roar fades into the distance. "We need to talk—"

"I think he sprained my jaw," Brody says, gingerly moving his lower jaw from side to side. "I'm gonna require serious makeup for news team next week."

"We need to talk." I bend down in front of him, trying not to grind my teeth in frustration at his superficial focus. Guess that's another thing Quince was right about. I'll add it to the list. "First, let's get you on your feet."

He grumbles but holds out his arm, inviting me to help him up.

Once he's standing—and repeatedly pressing against the corner of his mouth, as if fascinated by the sensation of a bloody lip—I place my hands on his shoulders.

"Brody," I say confidently, "look at me."

I've never performed a mindwashing before—I've never had to. But every mer in the sea is required to memorize the ritual, just in case something like this happens. The first step is establishing eye contact, creating and then maintaining the visual connection.

When Brody's golden-brown eyes meet mine, caught by the hypnotic glitter of my magical focus, I take a deep breath and recite the words in my mind.

260

What was seen is now forgotten,
What was learned is now unknown.
Memories made are all but rotten,
New replacements shall be shown.

As soon as I finish the last thought, Brody blinks rapidly and shakes his head. Confusion fills his features, making him look completely lost.

I almost feel bad. Brody, the boy who always seems at home in every situation, looks totally disoriented . . . because of me. Well, it's not like I had a choice. I couldn't exactly leave him knowing the secret. I have no idea what he would do with that information. For all I know, my kingdom and I would become his next news-team exposé.

"Lily?"

Taking a deep breath, I plunge into a story to explain the situation.

"Are you okay, Brody?" I ask, feigning serious concern. "You took a hard tumble down those steps."

He glances back over my shoulder, looking at the steps in question and trying to put the pieces together in his mind. Trying to fill the gaps I made in his memories.

"I fell?"

"Yeah," Shannen says, climbing out of her car and coming to my aid—love her! "You came out here to ask Lily something about your next race and just—"

"—took a header into the parking lot," I finish.

While Brody shakes his head, Shannen and I share a look. She looks totally proud of herself . . . and of me. I'm pretty proud of me too.

"Let me help you inside," I offer, slipping to his side and wrapping an arm around his waist for support. "Coach will know what to do."

"Oh. Okay," Brody mutters. "Yeah. Coach can help."

As I escort Brody to the steps, I look over my shoulder and tell Shannen, "I'll be right back."

I can already feel the migraine starting right above my left eye. If I try to stick it out for the rest of the meet, I'll be incapacitated for a week. No, I'll get Brody into Coach's hands, then it's home for a double dose of aspirin and a long nap in a dark room.

Quince will have to wait until tomorrow.

The migraine is still raging the next morning, so I skip school. By the afternoon, though, it's dissipated to a dull ache, and knowing tonight's the night we return to Thalassinia, I'm sitting on my front step waiting for Quince when I hear his motorcycle rumble in the distance.

I shake off the melancholy thoughts I've been wrestling with all day and paste on a happy smile. As he pulls his bike into the driveway between our houses, I think I've actually managed to conjure some happiness.

Clearly, Quince is not fooled.

"You weren't in school," he says as he climbs the steps to

sit next to me. "You okay?"

"Sure," I say, pretending it's true.

He turns his bright eyes on me. "Seriously, Lily. Are you all right?"

His sincerity shatters my façade. I'm not all right, I want to scream. I'm as far from all right as I can get because I'm sad and confused and I don't know what to do.

But that's the emotion talking—or thinking. The reality is a little more complicated.

"I'm disappointed in myself," I say finally. "All these years wasted on loving Brody . . . and it was all a fantasy. Just like you said."

"Yeah, well, you had to realize that for yourself." Quince puts an arm around my shoulders and hugs me to his side. And even though he happens to be the most confusing thing in my life at the moment, I let him. At least he's not saying "I told you so."

I say it instead. "You told me so," I admit. "You told me my image of Brody wasn't real, and you were right. I was just too blind to see it."

He laughs a little. "You were too blind to see a lot of things, princess."

It's reassuring when he calls me princess—as opposed to *Princess* or, worse, Lily. One seems too mocking, the other too intimate. His ironic nickname feels safe.

I look down, away, and see his bruised left hand— knuckles scabbed over now—braced on the front of the step. Great white shark, how had I forgotten about the fight? Too wrapped up in my own issues, I guess.

"Did you break anything?"

He looks at me with raised brows, and when I nod at his battered hand, he frowns. "No. The idiot might need an ice pack or two, but nothing requiring medical attention."

I can't help it. I burst out laughing at the fact that Quince thought I was asking about Brody.

I lean across his body and lift his hand for inspection. As I run my fingertips over his broken skin, careful not to cause more pain, I say, "I meant you, blowfish. *Your* bones."

His hand trembles a little in mine. Somehow, that rattles me more than anything else. I could deal with losing my fantasy Brody more than I can face a very real, trembling Quince.

"No," he whispers. "I pulled my punches." Then, with some of his usual humor, he adds, "Principal Brown already thinks I'm one step away from juvie. Don't need to put myself there."

I look up, ready to argue, when a lumpy spot in his heather gray T-shirt catches my eye. Lifting my fingers to the place just beneath his collarbone, I'm both surprised and not to feel a sand-dollar-shaped object. My gaze continues the journey up to his.

"You're still wearing it."

We both know it's not a question, just like we both seem to have lost the ability to breathe. A whole sea of emotions

264

washes through his eyes—fear, anger, pain, trust, love. Love. It's when I see that last one that I close my eyes.

He whispers, "Always."

That's what I was afraid of.

My confusion rushes back, shoving all other thoughts aside. I pull away, staring down at my hands folded tightly in my lap. I'm not ready for this, not ready for him. I can't be.

"Quince, I—"

"I get it, Lily," he says, my name giving more weight to his words. "Really I do. You've been through a lot in the last two weeks. I know you need some time to process."

I feel like relief should sag through me, but it doesn't. Still, I say, "Thank you."

"But," he says, his voice shifting back to the strong, powerful Quince, "that doesn't change how I feel. How I've always felt. I care about you, Lily. I—"

"Stop!" I can't hear the words he is about to say. My mind is muddied enough already, without his feelings coming into play. But when I imagine the hurt in his eyes—eyes I can't look into right now—I add, "I'm sorry."

"It's okay," he insists. "I don't have to say the words. You know."

Yeah, I do. And that just makes everything a million times worse.

"Are you ready to go back to Thalassinia?" I ask, needing to take some action to make this confusion, this ache in my chest, go away.

Now I finally do look at him, and he's studying me. He's got his thoughts carefully masked, though, so I can't guess what he's going to do until he says, "Sure. Just let me go tell Mom I'll be gone."

As I watch him walk across the lawn between our houses, I think I should feel more relieved. The mess of the bonding, the muddle of magic and emotions and royal expectations, is finally going to be over.

Hopefully, by the time we get to Thalassinia, I'll have decided what I'm going to do.

22

*A*s we reach the outskirts of Thalassinia, I've slipped into delay mode. I still haven't made my decision, and I need a little extra time to think. Although, with emotions involved, it's not like thinking is going to be a major help, but it can't hurt to try. So I do something I've never done before. I take someone to my secret spot.

We're getting closer and closer to summer, so there is still plenty of sun filtering through the waves as we swim into my sacred retreat. My personal haven.

Quince seems to sense the awe-inspiring nature of this place, because he doesn't say a word, just looks around at the bounty of colors and textures and contrast that fill my spot. Then, as if he knows how I spend my time here, he corkscrews onto his back and gazes longingly up at the sky. At the world above the surface.

The world where he belongs. And I don't.

I float up next to him, pondering that thought. It's something I've always believed, even after I found out Mom was human and I have family on the mainland. I'm a Thalassinian princess, and my place is beneath the sea. Below the surface.

A tiny fishing boat passes overhead, its bright red hull shining like a stop sign in the reflected light from the reef below. I feel Quince tense, probably thinking of the last fishing-boat encounter, but I lay a reassuring hand on his arm.

"It's fine," I say. "A lot of fishing boats travel this route between Bimini and Nassau. They won't be stopping to drop line."

"Oh," he says, the word somehow full of self-mocking. Like he feels foolish for worrying.

"But it's always better to be on alert," I say, mostly to make him feel better. "You never know when the current will change."

We float in silence, watching as the red boat passes out of view and a yellow follows shortly after, then turquoise, magenta, and bright, bright green. A rainbow parade.

"There are so many colors in the sea," he says, his voice full of awe. "Makes me feel kind of out of place in my gray cargo pants."

Something about that statement twists my heart into a knot, but I ignore the ominous feeling.

"Your eyes," I say, picturing them from memory. "They are the color of the sea. They've always reminded me of home."

They're the only part of him that seems to belong here. Everything else—from the earthy blond of his hair to the impressive muscles and rough calluses earned through hours of working on his motorcycle and at the lumberyard—screams land. He—I start blinking too fast—is made of the land.

"What's wrong?" he asks, as if instantly aware of my thoughts.

"Nothing," I insist. "I just—"

He floats up so he can look at my face. "Your eyes," he says, his voice awed. "They're sparkling. Glittering like they're painted with tiny gold diamonds."

Oh, no. Well, I can't wipe at nonexistent tears, so I change the subject.

"This is my secret spot." I force myself to stop blinking so fast. "It's my favorite place in all of Thalassinia. In all the seas."

Quince scowls for a second, like he's not buying my distraction, but apparently decides to let me have it. Twisting back skyward, he says, "I can imagine why. It's beautiful."

Then, I don't know why I say it, don't even think the words before they spill out of my mouth, but I say, "I've never shown this place to anyone before."

Quince freezes, still looking to the surface. "No one?"

I shake my head, even though he might not be able to see me.

"I'm . . ."

I feel his pleasure before he says it.

" . . . honored."

It is such a painfully sweet moment that I almost can't bear to end it. If only we could just stay here, in this world between worlds, without royal obligations, motorcycles, or bad memories. But I can't. It's all ending.

"I'm glad you appreciate it," I say softly. "Because after tonight, you will never be able to come here again."

And with that, I've sealed our fate. My decision is made.

Despite my confusing feelings for Quince—not that I can trust my feelings lately—and his increasingly obvious feelings for me—I'm going through with the separation. I don't think I have another choice.

"Think about what you're doing, Lily," Quince pleads.

We're sitting outside Daddy's office, waiting for his staff to prepare the ritual. Daddy's face fell when I told him my decision, but he didn't argue. Maybe he could tell that I was not about to be persuaded.

Quince, on the other hand, still thinks he can change my mind.

"You know how I feel about you," he says. "And I think you're starting to feel the same way about me."

"That doesn't matter," I insist.

270

"The hell it doesn't." He slams a fist against the smooth pumice bench and is probably disappointed when the water muffles the effect. "Lily, I love you."

"No—"

"I know you don't want to hear that, but I do." He swims awkwardly in front of me, taking my shoulders in his hands, like if he can just make me look at him, I'll see how foolish I'm being.

But looking into his eyes only makes my decision easier. Because his eyes are full of a certainty I'm not sure I will ever have.

Yesterday I was head over fins about Brody, and look how well that turned out. I had deluded myself into believing an infatuation was true love. I was ready to commit myself to a lifetime with a boy I barely knew.

How can I be sure that these feelings that are churning for Quince are any more real? Any less imaginary? They might be real. Or they might be symptoms of the bond or a reaction to Brody or just a result of spending so much time together.

And how, if they *are* true and real, could I allow him to sacrifice everything he knows—his friends, his family, his motorcycle, his future—to spend most of the rest of his life in the ocean?

"Lily, you can't just throw this—"

"I have to," I cut in. "*We* have to. Be logical, Quince. If we don't separate, then by the next lunar cycle the bond will

271

finalize and you will turn fully mer. Your terraped form—your legs—would be permanently tied to mine."

"I know that. Your cousin explained the whole thing." He rolls his eyes. "Probably thinking it would scare me off."

"You would never walk on land without me again."

"So—"

"When I take my place in court, I'll have to be in Thalassinia almost all the time," I explain, trying to hit this home for him. "Think about that. Think about being stuck in the ocean most of your life. Not being able to ride your motorcycle whenever you want. Not being able to run or dance or climb a—"

"I don't dance." He is still not getting it. "Lily, I've spent the last three years crazy over you. I don't want to let this chance slip away. Especially not now that I've seen what things could be like with us."

Aaargh! He's being obtuse. "What about your mom?" I ask. "Who would go to the grocery store for her or take out her trash or fix her junker car when she's late for work?" All things I know Quince has done. Guess I have been paying attention.

The thought of having to abandon his mom actually gives him pause. Good! He needs to be thinking about stuff like that.

But then he shakes his head. "We can work that out later. I'm willing to make those sacrifices. Why can't you see that?"

"You might be," I shout, my emotions flooding out. "But I'm not."

"I don't—"

I have to say something to make him understand. The truth won't work. I can't tell him that I hate the thought of him sacrificing everything in his life to be with me . . . only to regret the sacrifice later. If I tell him that, though, then he might realize that my feelings for him are growing, and he'll use that as the anchor in his argument. If he knows that I even *think* I might be falling for him—and what if I'm just as wrong about these feelings as I was about Brody?—he'll never let go.

And I couldn't live with that.

We're from two different worlds. He belongs in his. I belong in mine.

So I say the only thing I know will make him let go.

"I'm not willing to give you the rest of my life." I shrug his hands off my shoulders and cross my arms. "I don't want you here."

I see the hurt in his eyes for an instant before he shuts me out. His eyes, his whole face, go blank.

He doesn't speak, just kind of floats away.

The door to Daddy's office opens and Mangrove swims out. "His highness is ready to begin."

Quince follows him into the office, leaving me alone in the hall. I take a moment to steady myself, to take a deep breath and tamp down the urge to cry. It's what has to be done.

And the reason I have to do it is the same reason that makes it so very, very hard.

"You are certain?" Daddy asks.

The question is supposed to be for both of us, but Quince doesn't answer. We both know Daddy's really just asking me. I nod, not trusting my voice. From the pained look on Daddy's face, I can tell that my eyes are sparkling. I can't help it anymore.

Daddy motions his guards forward, and they take position at either side of Quince.

"Then, by the power vested in me by the great sea god Poseidon," he says, gripping his trident in his right hand, "I declare this bond . . . irreversibly severed."

I feel a spark of electricity tingle over my skin. All at once, it feels like every last one of my emotions drains from my body.

Cid, at Quince's left, grabs him by the arm and says, "Take a deep breath, son."

He does—his last breath of water—and Cid and Barney kick off through the open window behind Daddy's desk, with Quince's now fully human body dragging between them. Once they clear the frame, I hurry to the window and lean out, watching, empty, as they rush Quince to the surface.

How can the right decision feel, all at once, so very wrong?

"It's not too late," Daddy says. "Until he breaches the

surface I can call him back."

"No," I whisper, my throat tight. It wouldn't be fair. I won't let my selfish—and unreliable—emotions take his future away.

"You are so very strong, daughter," he says, pulling me into his arms.

Resting my head against his shoulder, I don't feel strong. I feel as opposite of strong as you can get.

I feel like a coward.

23

"Next," Daddy calls out to Mangrove.

His secretary goes off in search of the next parties seeking an audience with the king. And—Daddy reaches over and squeezes my hand—the princess.

"I am so very glad you decided to return home," he says for the millionth time since I returned for good earlier this week. "I missed you more than I can say."

I force a smile and try to ignore the part of me that wishes I hadn't said good-bye to Aunt Rachel last weekend. I'd been back on land for only a few hours after the separation before it became abundantly clear that I couldn't stay. Being so close to Quince, while feeling an ocean apart, was just painful after everything we'd been through. It was only four days ago, but it feels like forever.

Before I have to come up with some response for Daddy, Mangrove announces the next visitors—a pair of seaholders who have a dispute about the border between their properties.

I zone out.

After the separation, I should have known I couldn't return to Seaview. No matter how much I miss Aunt Rachel and Shannen, there was too much waiting for me there. Too much emotion. Too much pain. Too much . . . just too much.

Besides, I belong in the sea, on the throne, so why waste time playing around on land? I was only delaying the rest of my life. I need to stay in Thalassinia, find a suitable— nonhuman—mermate by my birthday three weeks from now, and prepare for my future as queen.

It's my duty.

"Very well, gentlemermen," Daddy says. "I don't expect to hear any more of these petty quibbles over a single inch of seascape. Understood?"

The two men nod enthusiastically and backpaddle out of the royal hall.

Daddy is so good at this. I know he's had most of a lifetime to practice, but somehow I don't think I will ever be as strong a ruler. And it doesn't help that, even though I'm sitting in the queen's throne—my mother's throne—and staring out over the lavish hall, all I see is land. Everything in Thalassinia reminds me of something on land. Of Quince.

I was waiting in this hall, right here in Mom's throne, when Quince came back from his tour with Dosinia. When they swam in, holding hands and laughing, I was so mad, I could have strangled them both. I guess everyone but me saw it for the jealousy it was.

I feel the tears tingle at the corners of my eyes. I need to get out of here before I start to sparkle. Daddy thinks I'm thrilled to be here, home and at his side. I don't want to disillusion him. I don't want him to know I'm just trying to forget.

Only I remember more each day. It's like the bond is still holding me to Quince.

"May I be excused?" I ask, more formally than usual because of the setting. Blinking my eyes quickly to stem the sparkling, I don't wait for Daddy to give his permission. As soon as I see him start to nod, I jet for the door.

Without going anywhere in particular, I swim through the hall and out the palace doors. As I cross the gardens, I remember Quince trying to ride the wakemaker—with little success. The excitement on his face made him look like a little boy on Christmas morning. In my memory, he looks up at me, his sea blue eyes twinkling, and smiles.

My eyes are probably shining like the sun by now.

Avoiding the palace gate—and the inquiring minds of the guards—I swim for the side wall, making it across and over into the relative privacy of life beyond the palace bounds.

Why is the right choice turning out to be so hard? Once the bond severed, setting Quince free for his land-based life,

I should have been able to go back to normal—or at least something close to normal. Maybe the separation didn't work? Maybe we're still magically connected and that's why I can't stop thinking about him. Can't stop feeling him, and feeling his absence.

Before I realize where I'm going, I'm knocking on Peri's front door.

Her mom answers, takes one look, and pulls me into a hug. "You poor dear."

"Sorry"—*sniff*—"Mrs. Wentletrap"—*sniff*—"I didn't know where else to go."

"Don't you worry," she says, soothing her hands up and down my back. Twisting her head toward the upper levels, she shouts, "Peri! Lily is here!"

I'm still crying on Mrs. Wentletrap's shoulders when Peri floats down. "Hey, Lily, I—"

I can just imagine what a mess I look like. Eyes sparkling with tears, hugging desperately to her mom, sniffling like a sick guppy. It's a testament to my sorry state that I can't even feel embarrassed for my complete and total breakdown.

"Oh, Lily," she says, floating closer and adding her soothing hand to my back. "What happened?"

I look up at her, feeling bleak and desperate and so very, very sad. "It's the bond," I wail. "Daddy didn't sever it right."

That has to be why, right? That has to be why I can't get

Quince out of my mind, even though we've been separated for days. Why I still feel a part of him in my heart.

"Sweetie," Peri says, all sympathy, "it's not the bond."

Sniff. "That's what Quince said."

"Mom, can you fix Lily a bowl of plumaria pudding?" Then, to me, "Let's go talk in the family room."

She leads me away while her mom swims off to the kitchen. Plumaria pudding is the undersea equivalent of chocolate. I don't think a mountain of it could make this pain go away.

When her mom is out of earshot, Peri says, "Tell me you don't love him."

"What?" I look up, startled. What kind of question is that? Well, not a question, but a weird request.

"Lily"—she lays her hand on mine—"I've known you longer than just about anybody."

I nod and sniff. We've been friends since almost forever.

"So that means I *know* you better than anybody."

Probably also true.

"Keep that in mind when I tell you," she says, "that I have never seen you as worked up about *anything* as you have been over Quince."

"Just because he likes to push my buttons," I say defensively. I know it's a weak argument.

Peri rolls her eyes. "You're not the most proactive girl in the sea," she says. "You defer to people when maybe you shouldn't, you take no action rather than create a potential incident. You take the safest course. I mean, you lusted after that guy Brody for how long without ever doing anything about it?"

"I was—" I start to defend myself, to say I was waiting for the right moment, but then I remember that it doesn't matter anymore. Brody was a fantasy.

"Quince may push your buttons," she says. "But when he's around you . . . I don't know, you have a fire inside. You meet him head-on, when you cow to others. You don't back down from him."

I think about that. It's definitely true, I don't take any carp from Quince. Ever. He pushes and I push back.

I'm not like that in the rest of my life. I'm not a push-over, really; it's just that I don't see the benefit in turning something into a massive confrontation. With Quince, I'm always itching for a fight.

I always thought it was just a personality quirk that came out when I'm away from the calming effects of water, but maybe it's more than that. Maybe it's Quince who brings my emotions to a boil.

But is that a good thing?

"What does that mean, Peri?" I shake my head. "That he brings out the worst in me?"

She shakes her head slowly, smiling. "I think he brings out the *best* you."

The best me? That can't be right. What's so great about being an aggressive, confrontational person? I'd rather float off to the side than swim front and center. I avoid conflict in every possible way.

But maybe that's a bad thing.

I think of Daddy, deftly handling the squabbling sea-holders with authority and just enough regal force to make them rethink bringing their petty argument before the king. *That's* what makes him a powerful leader. He is confident in his decisions and dares anyone to defy him.

I'm not like that.

At least, not with anyone but Quince.

That's when it hits me. Peri is partly right. Quince brings out a fire in me that burns to take him on. With Brody— before I realized he was nothing more than imaginary perfection—I was afraid to do something wrong, something that would make him laugh at or ridicule me. With Quince, I've never had that fear.

With Quince, I don't feel like a lesser being . . . I feel like an equal.

With Quince, I don't have to pretend to be anyone other than exactly who I am. He makes me content to be me. That's what makes him my perfect mermate. Well, that and the fact that I love him to pieces.

"Peri, I—"

"I know," she says, giving me a gentle shove. "You have to go."

"I'll see you soon," I insist.

"Promises, promises," she says as I disappear out the front door.

I'm too busy worrying about what Daddy will say when I tell him I'm going back to Seaview. He will be so disappointed.

"I wondered how long it would take," Daddy muses as he studies the calendar on his desk. "Bet Mangrove ten star bucks that you'd be gone within two days."

"What?" I expected some kingly rage, a slammed fist or two. Maybe even a royal edict. I definitely hadn't expected a wager.

"Lily," he says, looking up at me with all the love he's always shown, "I'm not blind. I can see how much you love the boy."

"I—" At first I feel a little embarrassed to confess to my dad, but then I realize there's no point in pretending. Especially since that's why I'm here in his office in the first place. "I do, Daddy," I admit. "I do love him."

"That's what you never realized about the bond," he says. "It doesn't force feelings that are not already there. It might uncover emotions you weren't prepared to admit, but it can't make someone fall in love. That you did all on your own."

"Why didn't you say anything?" I complain. "You could have saved me—saved *us*—a lot of time and heartache."

"Would it have done any good?" he asks sagely. "You

weren't ready to hear the truth—from me or from Quince." He smiles. "Besides, I wanted you to realize for yourself what you wanted. In love and in life."

Life. Yeah, my life is definitely going to change. If I'm going back to be with Quince, then I'm facing a very different future from the one I've always imagined. With the bond immunity in place, he can never become mer. And it's not like humans can apply for a day pass to Thalassinia. He can't make his home in the sea.

Which means neither will I.

Which means I won't be taking my place in Daddy's court or preparing to succeed to the throne. Thalassinia can't exactly have an absentee crown princess in her court.

Strangely, the thought doesn't make me feel as sad as I would have thought. In fact, I feel a little . . . relieved.

"Daddy, I—I'm going back. To stay."

"I know." He shakes his head and smiles sadly. "I wish you had realized this before we conducted the separation." Then he huffs out a little laugh. "Although I think I've always known that your dreams reach far beyond this palace. You've never fully belonged to the sea, have you?"

"Maybe not," I say, even if it feels weird to say so. It's strange to realize that the place you've always considered home might not be where you're supposed to end up.

"You've always had more of your mother in you," he says. "She tried to convince me to move to land. Said she didn't think she'd ever feel entirely at home in a world where she might float away in the night."

"Did you want to?" I ask. "Move, I mean."

"Of course. I loved your mother more than anything in the world, until you came along."

It's such a sweet declaration that I swim over his desk and hug myself to his chest.

"But by the time we met, your grandfather had passed and I had already ascended to the throne." He squeezes me closer. "Leaving the kingdom was not an option."

His duty before his heart. And am I about to make the opposite decision?

"What about me?" I ask. "Thalassinia will lose its heir if I don't bond by my birthday."

And it's not as if I could bond to someone else, knowing that I love Quince.

"First of all," Daddy says, "I plan on living a good long time, so Thalassinia has plenty of time to find a new successor, if that's your final decision. We might be able to find a loophole around the bonding-by-your-eighteenth-birthday law."

I smile. I always had a hard time with the idea that I would take the crown when Daddy dies. It felt like I would be stealing it from him just when he was stolen from me. But I never allowed myself to think of what I would do if I weren't the royal princess. Maybe I'm destined for something else.

"Secondly," he continues, hopefully unaware of my sad thoughts, "neither your mother nor I would *ever* want you

285

to put your royal duty before something as personal as love. We want more for you."

This is why he's always felt more like a dad than a king. What royal daughter could ask for more?

"I love you, Daddy."

"And I love you, daughter." He gives me one last squeeze before holding me away from him. "Now, would you go after Quince already? I've had more of your tear-sparkled eyes than a merman can handle. The next time you visit, I want to see you as happy as you can possibly be."

Now that's a royal edict that I will gladly fulfill.

24

*W*hen the roar of Quince's motorcycle echoes through the neighborhood, I'm sitting on his front porch. Aunt Rachel is probably spying on me from the living room window—I've never seen her so excited as when I walked back into her kitchen. After a dozen minutes of smiles and hugs and happy tears—and Prithi happily lapping at my toes—I told her why I've decided to return. She quickly shoved me out the front door and told me to wait for Quince to get home from school.

I love her, but the woman can be a little pushy.

Quince still hasn't noticed me when he turns his bike into the driveway and heads for the back. As he coasts past the porch, he turns and stares wide-eyed at me.

But he doesn't stop his bike. The next thing I know, he's coasted out of sight and I hear the sound of a motorcycle crashing into something—probably the two metal garbage cans that Prithi is so fond of scavenging.

I jump to my feet, but before I can round the corner to make sure he's okay, he's standing there—right there in front of me—and it's all I can do not to fling my arms around his neck and kiss him silly.

The stormy look on his face holds me back.

"Lily?" he asks, as if he can't quite believe it.

It's only been a week.

But I know what he means.

Feeling a little self-conscious, now that I have to actually speak, I wave like a dork and say, "Hi."

Oh, brilliant, Lily. Frogging brilliant.

"What are you—?" He shakes his head. "I thought you were staying. Your aunt said—"

"I'm back." I just can't get enough of looking at him, of feeling him. All the parts of me that have felt empty for the last few days are suddenly flooded with him. With his strength and his pride and his big Caribbean blue eyes that always remind me of home. Just as he will always *feel* like home. "I decided to come back."

He doesn't look excited, though. He looks . . . suspicious.

"Why?"

"*Why?*" I repeat.

"Why did you come back?" His eyes are completely guarded. "What changed your mind?"

This is it, I think. The moment of truth.

Literally.

But the truth is a scary thing. Especially when it leaves you completely vulnerable.

"I missed the lip gloss," I tease. As soon as I say it, I know it's the wrong thing. This isn't the time for joking. Not only do I feel sour inside, but the guarded look on Quince's face turns to distance. I won't let him pull away.

"That's a lie," I confess.

He scowls in confusion.

"For you," I admit, every muscle in my heart panicking at the revelation. "I came back because of you."

"Yeah?" he asks, his confused look softening with a smile that crinkles at the corners of his eyes.

Willing myself not to faint before I can get the words out, I say, "I love you, Quince. I didn't want to stay away. I couldn't."

"Woohoo!" He shouts, closes the distance between us, and lifts me into his arms, spinning us around. "I knew it!"

Before I can respond with disbelief—he so obviously did *not* know it—he sets me down and takes my face in his hands. His lips are on their way to mine when he pulls back.

"Hey, I'm not about to set off another crazy magical bond again, am I?" Then, as if he just realized something, he says, "Not that I'm opposed or anything. I just want to be clear about what I'm getting into."

"No," I say, trying to shake my head. "No more bonds. You're immune now."

"Okay," he says. Then he finishes what he started.

His lips on mine feel so soft and warm and . . . perfect. Without hiding behind the magic of the bond—and with my feelings out in the open—I can recognize the true magic of our kiss. Quince said once that love is the strongest magic in the world. Now I know he's right.

When he pulls back, his eyes glow with the love I know is shining inside. I'm sure my eyes are glowing just as bright, because I can feel the tears of joy sliding down my cheeks.

For several long minutes, we just smile at each other. I'm sure we look like stupidly in love teenagers—to Aunt Rachel and whoever else happens to be watching—but we know the truth. There's nothing stupid about it.

"Now that you're back," Quince says, slinging an arm around my shoulders and leading me toward the driveway, "I'm going to teach you to ride Princess."

"Princess?"

"My motorcycle."

I laugh. "You named your motorcycle Princess?"

"What can I say?" he teases. "I call all my favorite things princess."

I take one look at Princess, lying on her side with two trash cans and a mess of garbage piled around her, and cringe.

"If you think I'm actually driving that death trap," I say, "then you're insane."

"She's safer than a wakemaker," he counters.

He has a point.

"Okay," I say, trying to be diplomatic, "I'll learn to drive Princess on one condition."

"Shoot."

"I get to wear a pink helmet."

He groans, like this is the biggest imposition ever. Finally he says, "Okay, but no streamers on the handlebars. She'd never live down the embarrassment."

"Deal," I say as I slip my hand into his and we start digging her out of the mess.

I bet I can renegotiate the streamers later.

Epilogue

*D*osinia Sanderson slipped through the open doorway to the king's office, her heart flutter-kicking despite knowing that the palace guard had retired when Uncle Whelk went to bed a few hours ago.

Still, the thrill of danger coursed through her. It wasn't fear of getting caught—she'd face whatever consequences the king threw her way—but excitement over what she was about to do. She'd pulled a lot of crazy and daring stunts in her sixteen years, but this was by far the boldest.

Having been an unwilling visitor here often enough, she didn't bother to snoop around. Muddy old scrolls and por-trait mosaics of her ancestors were about as exciting as sand. And just as useful. Instead, she headed directly for her prize. Perched on a stand behind the king's desk, like a hydra wait-ing for the ocean current to whisk it away to a new home, stood the royal trident. It looked common, useless. But in the hands of a merperson of royal descent it would wield great power.

It just so happened that Doe was a merperson of royal descent.

As she wrapped her fingers around the staff, she felt a small burst of electricity, a charge that tingled through her wrist and forearm. An ancient magic. Finally, she thought as she swam back out the way she'd come in, she would get her revenge on those responsible for her parents' deaths: humans.

Acknowledgments

*T*his book has been floating offshore for a long time, waiting to wash up on a sunny beach, so naturally I have a whole school of fish to thank.

Sarah Shumway (*Editorius fabuloso*)—A species of editor-fish with the cunning ability to pinpoint all the flaws of a manuscript in anywhere from five to eleven pages and to guide *Authora neo* in producing the best book possible.

Jenny Bent (*Agenta brilliantum*)—This particular species of agent shark has a natural instinct for negotiating great deals, keeping *Authora neo* sane during lo-o-ong waiting periods, and giving awards-ceremony-wardrobe advice.

Sharie Kohler (*Friendela prima*)—A loyal, supportive, and brilliantly talented species of friendfish. Can be particularly impatient, especially when waiting for a certain favorite mermaid book to finally come to light.

Kay Cassidy, Tina Ferraro, and Stephanie Hale (*Authoras*

palista)——Found in the Gulf of Facebook or the Twitter Sea, this species often stops personal activities to help *Authora neo* by reading rough-draft pages on short notice.

Blue Willow Bookshop (*Literati amorosa*)——A Gulf Coast coral that creates an ideal environment for *Authora neo*, forming a perfect symbiotic relationship. A tendency to squeal and gush serves to make it even more inviting.

Mom and Dad (*Parentos perfectos*)——The pinnacle species of parentfish that continues to support their child despite recurring phone calls on the topics of auto repair, purchase advice, hypochondria, and career-related neuroses.